# Gulfside Secret

## A HAVEN BEACH NOVEL

### REBECCA REGNIER

# One

## JOETTA PRESENT DAY

Joetta couldn't tear her eyes from the three beautiful women who stood before her. She knew their names. She knew what they sounded like before they even spoke. She knew their hearts when they beat inside of her. And yet... she didn't know them at all.

The room smelled of antiseptic and sweat, mingled with a hint of plastic.

Heartbeats. Joetta's was thumping so hard it felt like it was crashing into her ribcage with every pulse. But none of those heartbeats was the one that brought them together.

They all focused on Didi's heartbeat. Tenuous, erratic, weak. Didi's heartbeat was the closest to stopping.

Didi, that was the name the three younger women called Belinda. Belinda was Joetta's big sister, and she wasn't Didi until Jorge. Didi was the name Jorge gave her. Her brother-in-law always called her big sister Didi. Once Jorge dubbed her Didi, Belinda was shed like a turtleneck in June.

In Joetta's heart and mind, the woman in the bed was her sister, her other half by any name.

Didi looked ashen and small. It looked like the hospital bed was pulling her inside of it, drowning her. Didi was receding from life to death.

Didi was in real trouble.

That image pushed away all the others.

There were secrets she'd tried to keep. A life she tried to forget, and it was in this room. The sins of Joetta's past were here, staring at her, accusing her of things she could not defend. Joetta had no pretense, even in her own mind, that she was a good person. An innocent person. She was guilty, no defense. Just guilty.

But what did any of it matter if her sister died?

This was the first time Joetta had breathed the same air with these girls since she crashed the car. Since she crashed her entire life. A lifetime ago. Her disastrous past was crashing again, now into her meticulously crafted present. Her today life.

Hiding, denial, compartmentalization, justification. She was the queen of all of those things. She had to be.

The past felt threatening; it made her want to turn tail and run again.

But the present demanded her full attention. Here in this room, the most important thing happening was happening to Didi. No matter who was here or why, it was her sister who mattered. If her life was about to collapse in on itself, she needed Didi. Didi was her rock just as much as her husband, Banks.

Didi knew everything. She'd know how to handle these three women, what to say, what not to say.

Because there was no guide to follow. No roadmap to consult. Joetta was faced with her past—her mistakes, her failures—in the same moment she was faced with losing the one person who had helped her through it all.

The words *I'm sorry* felt meaningless. Her desire to know more about these three women was immense. But the fear that she would have to go through this now, without the rock of her life, was something she could barely comprehend.

*What to do next? What to say?* All of those things played in her mind—but the persistent beeping got louder. Didi's heartbeat.

Jorge made a sound. It wasn't a word; it was a cry.

That sound let her know that Jorge was feeling the same way she was. Despair, panic, and the frantic need to find someone to help Didi!

It was his voice that cut through the strange situation they found themselves in. Words formed from the cry, and Jorge yelled, "Help her!"

Jorge's plea pressed play on the action in the room. The slow motion that had trapped her voice and rooted her feet to the floor switched to fast forward.

There was no time for slow realizations or cautious greetings.

There was an immediate emergency. She scanned the bed for a nurse call button. *Where was it?*

"Help her!"

At the sound of Jorge's plea—yell, really—Joetta heard running footsteps getting louder from outside in the hall.

A team of nurses and doctors burst past the girls, blew past her like a high-speed train, creating a wind with their forward motion.

They went straight to the most immediate concern.

"We've got to take her back in," Joetta heard one of the nurses say.

"Prep O.R. Six. Send another page—Dr. Winston, immediately!"

The past would have to be reckoned with. Joetta knew that now. The cat had crawled out of the bag. It had claws and teeth.

But right now, all that really mattered was the present—and making sure that Didi's heart kept beating.

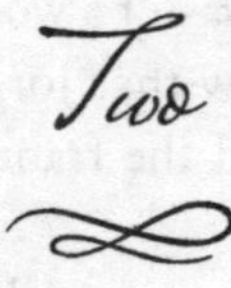

## Two

## BLAIR

Blair filed in last.

She saw the woman, who claimed to be their mother. She saw her. She felt Ali grip her hand. And then, they were all ushered out in confusion.

She held fast to Ali and Faye as the swirl of nurses and tubes and sounds nearly overwhelmed her senses.

She hadn't met Didi or Jorge, but somehow, she knew who everyone was. Faye and Ali had told her stories of the beach, of the lovely old couple who managed The Sea Turtle. She had also heard stories, a precious few of their once long-lost mother.

It was easy to put a name to each of the faces despite the surreal scene they were all in.

But just as fast as the nurses came, they were all ushered out of the way.

The woman who was clinging to life needed all the air in the room. All the attention. They couldn't help; they were in the way.

One minute, they were in the middle of a hospital room, and the next, they were in the waiting room.

Blair registered the older man's distress, Jorge. He loved his wife, Didi, and she was in grave danger. The poor man! Their bond was almost a physical entity. Wow. *What must that be like? To find your person?*

Ali let go of Blair's hand and went over to Jorge. She heard Ali say, "What can I get you?"

Jorge shook his head. "No. Nothing."

Faye hadn't said a word.

And the woman—the one who claimed to be their mother—stood silently, her eyes wide. She looked like a cornered animal.

Blair had no memory of having a mother. Not ever. Her entire life.

She felt a little jealous of Faye and Ali's memories. So much so that when they told stories about "Mommy," Blair liked to pretend she remembered too. But she didn't.

All she saw right now was a stranger. A beautiful woman who looked scared. On that level, Blair and the older woman were plucking the same guitar string.

She was scared, too.

Blair had just left her entire life. She didn't know if Blake was coming after her. She hadn't told Blake that she was pregnant.

After years of thinking she wouldn't really be able to get pregnant, here she was. Her cycles were never regular, and she'd had myriad other issues over the years, plus she was over forty. Perimenopause was a much more likely cause for her symptoms at this age. But there was no doubt. She was going to have a baby.

Without thinking about it, Blair put her now free hand over her stomach. She was protecting it.

She was going to be a mother, too.

Maybe this was divine timing. Maybe as she was going to become a mother, she needed a mother. Her feet moved just as instinctively as her hand had. And she honestly didn't know why she did the next thing she did—but Blair walked forward and put her hands out toward the woman who said she was their mother.

She looked at the woman. She was blonde like Ali. Blue-eyed like Ali. The same size, even, as Ali. Ali was of this woman, no question. Faye was a Kelly through and through, but Ali and this lady were a pair. That was striking. Maybe Blair was a combo of Bruce and this woman? Who knew?

"Mommy...my name is Blair."

The woman sucked in air as if it were a jagged, toxic thing.

"I know," she breathed. "I knew that."

And all of a sudden—out of nowhere—Blair was in the woman's arms. They were hugging.

No matter what else happened, no matter what had happened before...Blair knew, down to her bones, this woman was their mother.

There was nothing to forgive—because there was no memory. Ali and Faye had a past with Joetta Armstrong, that was her name. Blair did not.

She had never had a mother.

But maybe now...she did.

It was her instinct—her only reaction—to connect with a scared person who had just entered their orbit.

This woman was bound to face a lot of wrath from Ali and Faye. They had memory, they had loss, they had decades of hurt.

But Blair didn't care. She was going to have her own relationship with this woman. Her own memory, not her sisters' stories.

Blair and Joetta hugged one another.

The rest would sort itself out.

# Three

## FAYE

Faye was used to taking her cues from Ali because Ali was in charge. But right now, Ali's cue to Faye and Blair was to help Jorge.

Ali wasn't paying attention to the woman who had dropped a bomb in their lives. It was as if Joetta didn't exist. Like it had always been.

Faye listened to Ali talk to Jorge.

"Jorge, we're here for you. She'll be OK. She's in good hands."

Ali always knew how to handle an emergency. She handled all their emergencies.

Ali didn't look toward their mother again. She kept her eyes fixed on Jorge.

She was focused on anything but their mother.

And then Faye watched as Blair hugged Joetta, their alleged mother.

Faye had questions, so many questions, and she had beef, for sure, against this woman who—poof!—was gone, and—poof!—was back.

But one thing they had promised on their way here to Didi's hospital room was that they would stay calm.

Ali had made them swear to keep the family drama out of the hospital so that the doctors could handle Didi's dire medical condition.

Faye took Ali's lead, as usual. She did not point a finger at Joetta and ask her what kind of person she had to be to have left her three daughters?

Faye tapped into a well of calm. She knew her mouth could get her in trouble, and it had. So, in this moment, her only play if she had a hope of keeping her promise to Ali was to clamp her jaw shut.

The absolutely impossible message that they had gotten from Didi, it turned out, was true. Part of Faye thought maybe Didi was just delusional or doped up on drugs before a medical procedure. But no. Standing in the waiting room was Didi's younger sister, Joetta. Joetta Kelly? Or Armstrong? Or Joetta-whatever?

Faye was going to have to stay cool and stay remote. This woman, who'd been with them so briefly but cast a shadow on them that lasted their entire lives, was so little, vulnerable even. Faye couldn't help but look at her, take in details about her.

But Faye wasn't looking for a mother.

Faye wasn't the point here, and she knew it. Blair was pregnant. Ali was concerned with Didi and Jorge. Faye knew she was the middle child, a supporting player in this drama, and she didn't want to blow this situation up any more than it already was.

And even Joetta wasn't the emergency. She'd been out of their lives for decades. She didn't get to be the center now. Joetta Whoever looked like she was used to commanding the focus. Was this really the person who lived only in Faye's memory?

The woman here, now, wore a navy-blue Ann Taylor sweater set and delicate gold jewelry. Her hair was slick and blonde and smoothed behind her ears.

Mommy wore clothes like an artist, that's what Faye remembered. Mommy tied bandannas over her hair.

Mommy's soft skin was stretched tightly over bone. Faye remembered Mommy was beautiful but out of place in her own neighborhood. That woman was unhappy—that's what Faye remembered. She was sad, chaotic, and beautiful, certainly.

The woman in front of her now was also beautiful, yet older, cultured, pulled together. But she looked scared. Terrified, actually. That frisson of fear felt very familiar.

Blair turned to Ali.

She knew that if Ali were in her right mind, she'd be making everyone feel better in this awkward moment. Ali would smooth it over.

But Ali had decided her priority was Jorge. That was where Ali had directed her energy; she had clearly decided to ignore the Joetta in the room.

Faye pretended she was Ali—and took charge of the situation.

"Ma'am," Faye started.

"You can call me Joetta." Her voice was familiar; was it because she sounded so very much like Ali, or was it the voice she heard in her dreams? Faye shook off the questions reeling in her brain. She channeled her inner Ali —the cool cucumber who fixed all things.

"We've had quite a shock, and I know who you say you are, but we're all concerned for Didi right now. And we are concerned for Jorge. So, if you're going to stay, we'll go. Let's do this in shifts, for Didi—"

That's where Joetta stood straighter. The uncertainty in her eyes changed completely.

"I appreciate it. But that's my sister, and I won't leave until I know she's OK."

Faye connected to Joetta in that moment. She put herself in the same position. If Ali had a medical crisis, would Faye leave? Never.

It was this woman's place to stay. And theirs to go. If they were going to honor their vow to keep things calm for Didi and Jorge, they'd need to go.

"I understand," she said to Joetta.

Faye went over to Jorge and Ali.

"If you need us, we're going to be at The Sea Turtle. Ali, come on."

Ali looked at Blair and Faye, but she refused to look at Joetta.

"Jorge, does that sound OK?" Ali asked Jorge, and he nodded. This drama could wait. His wife was his focus, as it should be.

"OK, let's go. We're a call away. And we'll be back in shifts if needs be," Ali asserted. But Faye didn't see Joetta leaving anytime soon.

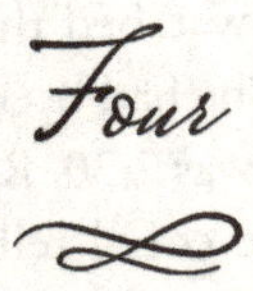

# Four

**1983**

## Ali

Ali sat in the nurse's office. She *knew* this was bad. Every time she tried to move, her arm throbbed.

It was an icy day at school. She and the rest of the children had been allowed to go on the playground. When she got off the swing set, she let go of the cold metal chain. She put her foot down on the snowy parking lot that served as the playground—and she slipped.

She fell forward, her arm under her body. She heard a snap. She didn't cry, but she *knew* this was a little bit more than a bruise.

Her teacher at Old Orchard Elementary had her sit in the office. And wait. They'd called Mommy.

Mommy wasn't going to be OK with all this.

Ali waited quietly. She didn't cry.

Mrs. Ollie, the school secretary, reassured her, "Don't worry, honey. Your mommy is on the way."

*On the way.*

Ali knew this could be bad.

"I really am OK."

"No, you're not. I think it could be broken. The doctor needs to look at it. Your mommy will take you to the doctor."

More time passed. She watched the black hands on the white wall clock move so slowly. She had been sitting in the nurse's office for two and a half hours. It was 2:30. Recess had been at noon. She was proud of how well she could tell time. It helped her get to school without tardiness.

Finally, there was her mother.

Mommy tripped on her way into the office. She looked beautiful, as always—but she also looked like she needed to comb through her hair. She needed to put the seams of the shoulders of her blouse *on* her shoulders. Everything was slightly off about her.

Ali knew why. The nurse also knew.

"Mrs. Kelly," the nurse said.

Ali's mother rushed to her side and kneeled down next to her. She put her arms out and drew Ali toward her.

Ali winced. Every motion hurt.

"I need to be—"

"Let's get you to the doctor right away. Here's your backpack." Ali couldn't reach out to get it. Her mother didn't see that. Mrs. Ollie did and took it instead.

"We'll put your work in it, and you can have it later. I suspect you're going to be absent for a day or two." Ali didn't want to be absent. She was trying for perfect attendance. She'd get an award at the end-of-year assembly if she had perfect attendance.

Ali stopped as her mother tried to hustle her to the door. She had to tell her teacher about her work.

"Will you please tell Mrs. Barr that I won't miss the homework assignment? I don't want to miss the homework assignment." Mrs. Barr was her art teacher. She was almost done with the bird drawing project. She loved finding the birds and drawing them.

"Honey, don't worry about that. Your teachers will understand," Her mother interrupted her. Mommy didn't understand how much work she'd done on her project.

The nurse at the school looked worried. A lot of grown-ups made that face when they saw Mommy. Ali hated that, so she put on a brave face; there was nothing to worry about. If Mommy didn't know what to do, Ali did!

Mommy helped Ali get into the car, the front seat. Mommy ran around the other side and got behind the wheel of the station wagon.

"Mommy, please drive slowly."

A flash in her mind—what if they got into a car crash and no one knew that her arm was already hurt? What would they do then?

Her mother started the car.

"I forgot—are we going to the ER? Or are we going to the doctor?"

"I think we need to go to the emergency room. You know the hospital on North Cove—it's right down the road. Turn on Kenwood." Ali answered with confidence; she was used to explaining these things. She knew every street in her neighborhood. She rode her bike and walked and remembered. This wasn't the first time she had to tell Mommy how to get somewhere.

Mommy hit the curb as they turned right onto Kenwood from Cheltenham. Ali knew the hospital was only a few blocks away.

Ali wished she would've walked it.

Her mother wasn't used to being anywhere at this time of day.

"Who's watching Faye?"

"Oh, don't worry. The neighbor's home. She saw me leave. She'll deal with Faye."

"Faye will be done with kindergarten in another half an hour."

"She'll walk home. I left the door open. She should be fine."

Her mother parked the car next to a big red sign that said *ER* and got out. She tripped and fell, and an ER nurse and an orderly ran to her mother and surrounded her.

They put her mother in a wheelchair.

They raced off, taking her mother into the ER.

Ali didn't cry—not in that moment. Her arm did hurt, and she understood a doctor needed to fix it. But she knew she had to take care of this—like everything else—on her own.

Crying wouldn't help. And neither would Mommy, who was pointing back at her.

## ALI
### Present Day

The memory of the last time Ali and her mother were in a hospital flashed in Ali's mind.

Her spine stiffened as she looked at her mother.

Ali had watched the video Didi had sent. She had promised Jorge not to make a scene, but the woman who walked into the waiting room was her mother. How could it be her?

But it was her.

Ali didn't really believe Didi or Jorge until that moment.

When Joetta Kelly—or whatever her name was—walked into the hospital room, Ali knew the truth. The awful, confusing truth. The truth that uncovered so many years of lies.

The woman was older. She was also immaculately put together. Mommy was always disheveled. That was an argument against this woman being their mother.

But there really wasn't a debate. She was the size Ali remembered. She even held herself like the mother of Ali's memory. It wasn't until she spoke that Ali felt the jolt go through her body.

That was her mother's voice.

Except this woman was neat. This woman was held together.

This woman in front of her was *not* the physical chaos that Ali remembered.

But no matter what her grooming or outfit looked like, it was her *presence* that caused chaos. This woman was a tornado of chaos, and in that, it was classic Joetta Kelly.

That was Mommy.

Ali remembered the promise she made to Jorge.

She didn't know Didi's role in all this, or her part in the lie.

Ali loved Didi and Jorge—even if they'd lied. Right now, that was not important. What was important was surviving the next few moments, hours, days, and sorting this out when Didi was better. Ali knew what it felt like when someone constantly made it about themselves; it was exhausting. Ali wasn't going to be that person. She blocked any instinct to confront this woman who gave birth to them. She didn't deserve any of Ali's energy or emotion. Didi did, not Joetta.

"Jorge, let us know what you need. But it's crowded. You and Didi need space." Jorge was barely there; his heart was in the room with Didi.

Ali turned to the woman.

"I know you say—I know *who* you say you are. We'll talk about this at a more appropriate time. *Now* is not the appropriate time."

"Let's go," she said to Blair and Faye.

Blair and Faye looked from Ali to Joetta.

Something in Ali's heart snapped shut. Ali would protect the Kelly Sisters, not this manicured version of a ghost from the past.

This woman may be their mother, but she owed them more than she could ever pay.

Ali thought about that long-ago day with the broken arm—where she waited in the nurse's office, and the attendants took care of her alcoholic mother, instead of realizing the little girl with the broken arm was the reason they were originally there.

They would wait.

"We're going to wait elsewhere. I suggest you stay with Jorge. Blair, Faye—let's go." She repeated it, this time with even more of an edge to her voice.

Her two sisters, for a moment, were torn—but as they had always done, they listened to Ali and followed her out into the hallway.

"But don't you want to—?" Blair asked.

"Not now. Maybe not ever." Ali shut the door to her mother, a woman who pretended to be dead.

*She can stay dead*, Ali thought.

## BLAIR

Blair felt the need for a drink. It was that simple. Every part of her life was upside down. She was no longer with Blake. She'd left all her stuff in their apartment. She didn't know if her job was going to accept her request to work remotely. And she was in Florida.

On top of all that, the mother she never knew was alive and kicking!

Blair felt out of sync with her sisters, mostly with Ali, when they left the hospital. Ali was cold, businesslike. She didn't want to talk about Joetta Bennett. Their mother. That was her name before it was Joetta Kelly. Joetta Bennett Kelly Armstrong. Armstrong was her name now. Wow, there were a lot of names to figure out.

Ali got in her car and said, "I'll meet you at The Sea Turtle Inn. You're going to love it."

Blair stared at her, confused. *They had to talk about this! Their mom was alive!*

"What about—?"

Ali looked at her and said, "She's not our mother." Then she got in her car.

Ali, the one who always smoothed over everything, had pronounced the conversation over.

Blair forced herself to look out the window and not back at the memory of their mother in that hospital room. She was here, in one of the most gorgeous places she'd ever seen, and she needed to appreciate that. Was stress bad for her baby? Probably.

Faye drove them to The Sea Turtle, so Blair was able to take it all in. After months of pictures and FaceTiming, she was actually here in person! Even though the circumstances were less than ideal, the actual resort was about as postcard-perfect a place as she could imagine.

The whirlwind of the past two days receded for a moment as she looked at the magical little tropical oasis.

"Oh my gosh, this is the cutest thing I've ever seen," Blair said as they pulled into the gravel parking area.

She was glad that Blake, her brand-new ex, wasn't with her. All he would see was *dollar sign, dollar sign, dollar sign*. That was going to be another issue. She didn't expect him to give up on her —well, correct that, she didn't expect he'd give up on the idea of getting her to cash in on this place so he could fund whatever his next scheme was.

Right now, Blair was cash-poor, and her checking account was anemic. That alone might buy her some time from Blake, but it wouldn't put a roof over her head.

Blair needed to find a place to stay, fast.

She'd also have to get her name off the lease of her Cincinnati apartment, ugh. Too many details to deal with. Luckily, the Ali she knew took over.

"This is the Blueberry Bungalow. I know it's not perfect. There's a lot to be fixed, but the plumbing works, the fridge works, and the sheets are brand new."

They walked in. Blair figured this was what 1965 looked like in

Florida. There was paneling on the walls, funky linoleum floors in the kitchen, and she wasn't sure, but she thought she saw a lizard scamper out of the way when they entered.

But somehow, it felt right. She realized she had a smile on her face, for the first time in a few days.

Ali opened a few windows. Blair made sure the refrigerator was on.

"We can make a run to Publix. Or Moe's. Moe's is right around the corner. Give me a list and I'll get you some food," Faye offered.

"No, no, no. You guys have done too much."

Ali looked at her little sister. "I hear congratulations are in order."

Blair's smile disappeared. What was her sister going to say about Blair's current predicament? The baby sister had baby-sistered her life into a mess.

"Yeah, so about that…I'm unmarried and, finally, after years of wonky periods, I'm somehow pregnant. Oh, and Blake doesn't know. I left everything behind. I did get my cat, that's something. Quite the résumé." Her nephew, Sawyer, was supposed to be cat-sitting.

"Can you text Sawyer to bring Darla here?"

"A baby is always a blessing," Ali said. Ali was smiling now, and it was the first smile Blair had witnessed from her big sister since she'd arrived in the most unhinged moment of all of their lives.

Faye raised an eyebrow. Faye got it more than Ali did. Ali was always by the book. The term "baby daddy" probably made her skin crawl. But here Ali was, being open and supportive, and that was a huge relief. Her big sisters were the lifeboat she needed when she felt like she was drowning. They wouldn't let her. She squeezed her eyes shut and tried not to cry.

"Well, it doesn't feel like that," Blair replied.

"I understand. I was in your boat—unsure—when I was pregnant with Sawyer. It was the scariest time of my life. But I had Ali. And you've got Ali. And me."

The three sisters were together, and even though they'd had a strange morning with Joetta, this felt right. The three of them against the world. Well, the two of them helping her figure out the world. She needed that!

"I can't pay for this room; in fact, I need to call my landlord and get myself off the lease. Blake would happily have me pay the rent even though I'm here."

"Give me the number," Ali told her. "I'm going to handle that. And as far as this cottage goes, you own a third of it. You're not paying for anything. But yes, I've got to rent these out, eventually. It may be that you move to the Inn after I make sure it isn't going to collapse or something," Ali was warm, but all business again.

*Collapse? What was she talking about?* But Ali was on to the next item on the resort manager list of things to do.

"Did you see the lizard that crawled across the linoleum when we walked in?"

"Uh, yeah, my new roommate?"

"Sort of. We do have work to do here yet, so we can't quite rent them out yet. You can stay here until we figure out what's next."

Ali knew how to handle all of the things. That was the overriding fact of her life. Ali had it under control.

Her older sisters fussed over her, made sure she was comfortable, and then, only after they could see she was in need of a nap, left her to rest.

They'd be back soon with food for the fridge, and a million of other things she could handle herself but didn't have to when her sisters were there.

And to be honest, Blair was so tired all of a sudden. She could have plopped down on the bed and slept, but the beach was right there. Sunset was hours away. Her sister had said something about a grand finale. But she decided maybe the beach would be the perfect way to cleanse her mind—and forget about the fact that she could really use a drink right about now.

She put on a pair of shorts that still fit thanks to the stretchy fabric, pulled her Bengals t-shirt over her head, and grabbed her flip-flops. She walked the little path toward the beach. From the kitchen window, she'd seen the pretty water, and darned if she wasn't going to get a little salty before she did anything else. When in Florida...She kicked off her flip-flops and left them on the little porch. The porch needed painting. Poor Ali, so many things to deal with!!

A few steps later, Blair had her toes in the sand. It was hot. *Yikes!* She did a little sprint toward the water, and the cool ocean foam rolled over her toes.

"Oh wow. I get it," she said to no one in particular.

She decided to walk on the beach instead of having the drink she craved. A glass of wine would not be her new therapy. No. Her baby deserved her best self. She didn't, but her baby did.

Blair walked, and her eyes scanned the horizon. She watched the seabirds run away from the waves as the water gently swelled and emptied. Those little creatures timed the water just right.

Blair stopped worrying about Blake and the mess she'd made. She stopped worrying that she was almost forty years old with nothing to show for her life.

These thoughts were selfish; she had to be done with selfish. Moms were selfless, or that's what she imagined. How do you become a good mother when you didn't have a mother?

A few doors down from the funky cottages of The Sea Turtle, Blair noticed a gorgeous, and very modern, well, it was a mansion. That's all she could really call it. Sure, it was a beach house— because it looked beachy—but it was huge. She noticed several enormous homes. And then condo after condo.

She turned around and looked back at The Sea Turtle Cottages and The Sea Turtle Inn.

*Wow.* They really were one of a kind. Everything else here

looked overdone and meant for someone with a lot more cash than she had. Cash. The Sea Turtle. Babies. Rentals. And their mother.

No wonder she wanted a drink.

She took another deep breath and realized: if she was going to be a good mother, it started now with being a mother and taking care of her own body. She had someone to protect—and that meant protecting herself. And that meant trying to be healthy.

Blair walked a little longer and took deep breaths. The sea was different. The salt almost touched your tongue with each breath.

Being a good mother would start right now.

She hoped.

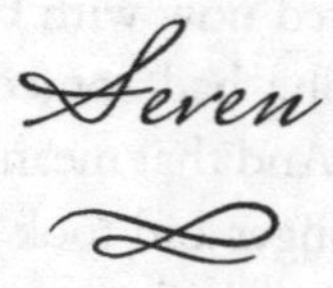

# Seven

FAYE

Faye and Ali needed a conversation. A big one. She texted Sawyer about getting Darla to the Blueberry Bungalow and then followed Ali.

In all of the upheaval that was Didi being sick and bundling Blair up to bring her to Florida, Faye had no time to think about the change she'd decided on.

Ali had changed her life, and now her sisters followed suit. What that what was happening? Did this happen to everyone after the death of a parent, this total weird shift of what you thought would be the future?

Faye wasn't introspective; she was more like Bruce Kelly than any of them, but still, she had changed her life. Upended it, really. Decades at the plant, and she'd decided—poof!—to join Ali in this Florida adventure.

Faye had no way to know if she'd made a mistake or the best decision of her life. Too much had happened in the last few hours to reflect on anything but one foot in front of the other.

Faye was used to sorting things out through gardening, and she'd put her garden and house in Ohio up for sale.

She knew she needed to get her hands in the dirt, and soon.

Blair had taken up so much of her thoughts—getting her out of her situation—that Faye hadn't really thought, since they'd traveled back down to Florida, about *her* situation.

But she'd made a decision. She was going to do the same as Ali. At least for now, she would be living in Haven Beach. Second-guessing herself wasn't in her nature. So, there it was, barrel ahead in the Sunshine State, come what may, even though, so far, what had come was bananas.

Faye did have to talk to Ali about how she fit in here, how she could help. That would be a much easier conversation than the *real* conversation they needed to have about their mother.

So, she decided to lead with that instead of the Joetta of it all. As Ali unlocked the office and grabbed towels and supplies for the cottage, Faye just blurted what was on her mind.

"I think I want to stay," Faye said. Ali's reaction was immediate and unequivocal.

Ali rushed to pull Faye into her arms. "Really? That's a dream come true. For us. For me. I thought you were just here because of the cataclysmic emergency. I never dreamed...Well, whatever brought you back, I'm thrilled. What changed your mind?"

"I just realized—between you and Sawyer and the unlimited plant-growing season—that I was meant to be here too. For now, at least. I feel like we can help each other do this." Faye waved her hands around to indicate "this" was the resort.

"Yes, we can," Ali said.

Ali was trying—within a year—to turn a losing business into a winning one. One that would support Ali, Blair, and Faye. Since Faye had been laid off from the plant, why *shouldn't* she stay and help Ali make it happen?

Ali hesitated. The brief burst of happy was gone that fast. Ali had a serious look once more.

"We're not making enough money to take money out yet. You understand that, right?"

"I totally understand that."

"I mean—we're living here rent-free, so that's a savings. But I'm not taking an income. I'm living off of my little inheritance from Dad, and my divorce settlement, not this place."

"I know and don't forget that I've got the buyout from the plant, and I'm going to sell my house and...and I'm going to find a job."

"There's plenty to do without you getting a job."

"I know. But I think between Sawyer and me and Didi when she's better—and Jorge—it's just good if I have gainful employment outside of the resort. We own this place, we don't work here as employees."

"That's true. What's the phrase about all our eggs in one basket?"

"Right, our rotten eggs need to get money from something other than this place until it's a cash cow. So many farm animal metaphors in one sentence." Faye laughed at her own turn of phrase.

"You'll be a boss here anyway, so you can come and go as you please." Ali was joking along with her. Ali had sold this idea hard, and it worked. They'd make it work together.

The word boss was weird to her. Faye had been a manager, sort of, at the plant—but never a *boss*. She hated bosses.

"You know, I'm not sure about that title. *Boss*. I'm used to being rank and file, you know?"

"Oh, please. You were one of the most upwardly mobile people at that plant."

"Yeah, but I mean—we're not wearing suits, right?"

"Well...bathing suits."

"Oh geez," they said together, and laughed again.

"I think I might be beyond my bathing suit days."

"Are you kidding me? You've got more muscle tone than any twenty-year-old."

"Well, that makes the gardening easier."

"So, what are you thinking, jobwise?"

"I'm thinking...It's time to call Mr. Palm Tree."

"For a job? Or for a date?"

"For ideas."

Ali knew that Faye and Rudy Palmer had a great time stand-up paddleboarding through the mangroves. She didn't know if Faye was ready to call that a date. She *did* know that when it came to finding a job, Rudy would be a good person to talk to. And she didn't mind having a reason to call.

"Presidential Suite still work for you?"

"Yeah. It worked for Sinatra. It works for me."

The suite was at the top of the hotel—the hotel that needed a lot of work to become a viable source of income.

"I hate to say it, but the Inn, that's gonna be a tough nut to crack, maintenance-wise," Ali admitted.

"I gave you that plan that your daughter and I worked out together. There's nothing to say that I can't work on that, little by little, while you continue to get the cottages ship-shape."

"I fear we need more than décor over there, but all we can do is work on it, right?"

"Right. So...the elephant in the room." By bringing up the weird fact that their mother was alive, Faye felt like she was ever-so-slightly sticking a toe in the water. Alive? She still couldn't really believe it.

"I don't want to talk about it. I *can't* talk about it. It could blow me apart to talk about it," Ali said to Faye. Ali was rarely this outwardly upset, or even negative. Ali didn't admit to needing help or even that anything was ever wrong.

This was more emotion than she ever showed, and she was trying to keep it in tight. Faye knew how much effort it took Ali, physically, to stay outwardly so even keel right now. So, Faye didn't push.

They would have to talk about it. And they would have to talk to their mother.

But right now, a million bombshells had exploded in the lives of the three Kelly Sisters. It was enough to know that they were all together. Faye took huge comfort in the fact that even though there were huge changes, for all of them, their bond remained the same.

# Eight

## BLAIR

Blair had never been much of a napper until recently. It was as if the blue line on the pregnancy test was her second confirmation that she was pregnant. The first? The nearly pathological need to nap. She'd taken a perfect one at the Blueberry Bungalow.

The breeze, the sea salt smell; it was the perfect setting for napping. Though admittedly, lately, she could nap anywhere.

Blair gently touched her middle.

"Is that you? Making sure I get rest?" She smiled. She had begun to have little conversations with the baby. Was she jinxing it? Was she putting the bassinette before the baby, to twist a metaphor?

After her nap and the strange few days, she had decided exercise was also a priority. Whatever she'd been getting from a glass or four of wine at night, she'd need to get from somewhere else.

And as much as she now needed naps, running was also her solace.

Blair needed to run. She looked it up—running was fine for

pregnant women. She was going to run. Neither of her sisters was into running like she was, but she felt like running kept her sane. Running kept her brain from spinning out of control.

She hadn't been running. She'd been drinking. And if she was going to successfully deploy Operation Good Mom, that meant good health.

Her sisters had told her that she simply must join them for the famous Grand Finale on the beach. There was a little time before she had to show up for that, so Blair decided the running would start now.

She'd run, shower, and be present and accounted for at this storied sunset soiree her sisters were so enamored with.

Blair knew some people ran barefoot on the beach, but it didn't seem wise. She liked a little bit of arch support from running shoes. Maybe if she were a permanent beach bum mom, she'd get better at barefoot running?

Blair laced up her running shoes, put on her sports bra, and pulled on a pair of running shorts. They were made with an elastic waistband, and only someone who knew her well would notice her bump.

Blair walked out of the door of the cottage and decided to take a right turn. At the very least, there'd be a lot to look at on this run.

She hadn't run in several months, so she figured if she could do a mile and a half today, she'd be doing good. She selected "running" on her Apple Watch and began with a nice, easy pace.

It felt funny at first, this different surface. She was used to running on the sidewalk and streets in Cincinnati, and when it was too-hot—or cold—the treadmill.

Soon her ankles got used to the surface. No such luck for her brain! Taking in this view was overwhelming. It really did look like paradise. As she ran, she looked down at the water. It was unbelievable, really, to be here. It felt tropical in a way that you didn't get in other places of the state.

"Why isn't everyone a runner here?" she thought as she

continued on. If she had this view and climate every day, it would be a crime not to appreciate it.

Blair felt really good, even though it had been such a long time. Her muscles remembered.

There was another runner up ahead. She had to figure that guy was a professional runner. He had the long, lean, muscular look of a marathoner.

Blair had done three marathons—not as many as some, but not nothing. She hadn't looked up what distance running recommendations there were for pregnant women, but she knew a mile, even a 5K, would be fairly safe.

The other runner, slightly ahead of her, gave her a pace to match.

She didn't know how long she had been running and realized it was probably far beyond the mile and a half she had wanted to do. The long-distance runner in front of her stopped, turned around, jogged in place for a moment, and headed towards her.

*"Oh geez, well I guess there goes the pace car,"* she thought.

She decided to let him pass her, and then she'd turned around too. That would make sense. As the runner passed her, they made eye contact. He smiled and gave her a nod.

*Wow. That was some smile,* she thought. *Are my hormones kicking in already?*

But he was handsome, his blonde hair and blue eyes made for the beachy setting.

Blair turned around to head back to The Sea Turtle. That's when her head, for a moment, felt like it was surrounded in gray fog—and she went down.

She had a slight spike of fear as she realized she was fainting! She hoped she hadn't hurt the baby.

Blair had no idea how long she was out, but she woke up to find that handsome runner hovering over her with concern and a bottle of water.

The nice stranger gave her his water. He seemed ridiculously concerned, and she had to force him not to call 911.

"It was like your legs turned to jelly," he said.

*Great.* She was mortified. And she also wanted to reassure him that she did not need an ambulance.

"I'm fine, truly fine." She was. As out as she'd been, she returned to consciousness just as quickly.

"Are you sure?"

"I'm sure."

She stopped short of saying what the problem was; she was pregnant and tried running for the first time in months on the beach in Florida.

He was a stranger, but his blue eyes looked kind, and then she blurted it out.

"I'm pregnant, so I guess this just sort of happens."

"Are you sure you're supposed to be running?"

"They say everything you used to do; you should be able to do."

But she knew that was true for young pregnant women. What about pregnant women in their forties? What about pregnant women who had just started working Alcoholics Anonymous? These questions she had not ask. She'd asked. She'd better find a doctor here, quickly, and start asking.

"Look, I'm not gonna call 911, but I'm at least gonna walk you home."

"To Cincinnati?" Blair replied with a laugh. She was making jokes to try to convince the worried stranger that she was fine.

"No, I mean to your hotel, or condo, or, well, I mean, I could get you to Cincinnati, but that would mean my private jet."

"Yeah, right, mine's in the shop, too. And I know, dumb joke. I kind of just moved here."

*Or ran away from home to here.* Somehow, life had got completely upside down.

"I live over there." She turned back from the water towards the shore, and there along the shoreline were the adorable little Sea Turtle cottages.

"Ha, we're neighbors. I always wondered what they look like inside." He said it as though he had concerns, and she was slightly defensive. Sure, the cottages were modest, but they were fifty times better than the cookie-cutter condos and mansions you saw everywhere in this state.

"Well, they're really cute," she said. "I just moved into one. Yeah, I kind of left a mess in Cincinnati."

"That sounds like a country song, if there ever was one."

Blair laughed. He was funny and had a nice face, a killer smile. She also checked herself; eligible bachelors that looked like him would not be in the market for geriatric pregnant women. And if there was one thing she was sure of, it was that she was an awful judge of boyfriend material. She banished those thoughts as quickly as they sprang up in her head.

"What do you know, that's my country music band name, Messy Cincinnati."

"Or a Kentucky Derby winner," he said. They had the same sense of humor, which was so rare.

"Cincy, you look a lot better—even after just passing out. But again, they take away my knight-in-shining-armor card if I don't make sure you get to your door."

Shining armor. She didn't need a knight. She didn't need anything shiny. She just needed to get her act together.

"All right." She stood up.

He offered a hand to make sure she was stable, but she was all better.

"I'm still walking to your door."

"How do I know you're not a serial killer?" she asked.

"Well, I guess I could be. But I think I probably would've put you in my trunk instead of giving you my water if I were."

"Fair point, you did have opportunity."

She realized she listened to way too many murder podcasts to have normal human interaction. That's why it was easy with a stranger. She didn't know why—maybe because they had no connection. No history. No expectation. Just a man—a handsome, nice man—who she had scared the crap out of. They walked slowly back to where she'd begun. He nodded to indicate she should be drinking water at regular intervals. Instead of protesting that she was perfectly able to manage herself, she actually took a sip every time. Her pride would not get in the way of Operation Good Mom.

"Here I am."

"Well, I guess my job is done."

"Thank you. In all seriousness. I'm sure I look scary."

"Well, you look beautiful. Like a beautiful, distressed—"

She cut him off. No need for compliments. She wasn't looking for a date.

"Beautiful? Distressed, I'll give you that. In fact, it's generous. I'm a total mess." Blair could only imagine what she looked like right now.

"Well, partial," he winked, and her hormones betrayed her again.

*Blair Kelly, you do not have time to flirt with strangers. Operation Good Mom, Operation Good Mom*, she repeated in her head.

"Well, rest assured, I'm fine. I've got family here. They will be fussing all over me, so you can stop."

"Right. But if I see you running out on the beach again, I shall be checking that you have water and rest times, Cincy."

"I will expect you to scold me next time I go running on the beach without proper hydration."

They parted ways, and Blair switched her focus to a good shower and a comfortable outfit for the grand finale. Before long, a light tap at the wood frame of the cottage door let her know it was nearly time to get out to the beach again.

"I've got your roommate here!"

Darla was curled up in Ali's arm, and she handed the kitty off to her.

"Darla! Did you have fun with Cousin Sawyer?"

"I think Sawyer would keep her if I didn't insist that you'd miss her too much."

"That is so true," Blair nuzzled her kitty's little head. She loved that spot.

"Come on, little sister. It's time for the grand finale."

"The famous grand finale."

"You got it."

"What does one wear for a grand finale?"

"Whatever one wants, dear. But comfort is the dress code."

That sounded good to Blair.

Ali was currently wearing a kaftan. Looking at her big sister right now, hair loose, kaftan flowing, you could almost believe Ali was footloose and fancy free. Ali was not fancy free, but she was putting on a good front for her two sisters. Ali was flappable; it just took a lot to flap her!

Blair decided to ask what she wanted to ask as she slid into a linen sundress that was loose and flowy and perfect for whatever size she was right now.

"So, the Mom sighting, you want to tell me what you're feeling? This had to be the shock of your life; it was mine."

Footloose and fancy free was stiff as a board at that conversational gambit.

"I told you I don't want to talk about it, and she's not our mom. She was never a mom to you at all," Ali said.

Blair got the picture. This was a non-starter. Ali did not want to be vulnerable. Did not want to talk about this. So, Blair let it go.

She also didn't tell her sister that she had completely passed out on the beach earlier in the day. There was no need to put more on Ali's list of things that Blair couldn't handle. A light jog on the beach should have been a no-brainer, yet Blair had bungled it. No need to tell Ali.

"Come on. Let's go," Ali said. Darla had found a perfect place to curl up on the couch. Satisfied that her cat was comfy, they left for the party.

Ali and Blair walked arm-in-arm to the center of the half circle of cottages that opened up straight onto the beach. Sawyer was there, joking with Faye. A handsome man who looked like Timothy Olyphant—*thank you very much*—was there too, pouring wine.

Ali explained, "My friend Erika usually comes for our little party; she runs the coffee shop across the street, but she's on vacation."

"This place seems like a vacation. Where do you go on vacation from vacation?"

"Actually, she went to Colorado to go ski," Ali explained.

"Well, that makes sense."

Blair then introduced herself to Henry, the handsome salt-and-pepper new face.

"Great to meet another Famous Kelly Sister!" he said. "Can I get you a glass of wine?"

She wanted a glass of wine. She wanted glasses of wine. But instead, she said, "Water."

"Can do!"

"Make sure she gets a pretty glass, though," Ali said.

"Yes, ma'am," Henry said, and he seemed to enjoy taking orders from Ali. Blair's former brother-in-law bristled at everything Ali said or did. It was refreshing to see her spend time with a man who appeared to appreciate her.

"Sit down. We've also got cheese, crackers. The local grocery store is my main supplier for the best components a charcuterie artist like me could ever want," Ali explained.

She was relaxed, despite the stress that had gone on the last few days—and there *was* stress. But there was something so easy about this. A couple more people wandered in and out, introduced themselves, and Sawyer seemed to be having a lighthearted discussion about ceramics. But no one was pushing Blair to explain anything. Even though she had a lot to explain. Like what had just happened in her life? What was about to?

"Look at that," Faye said to Blair, interrupting her conversation with Sawyer. "It's gonna be an orange one."

And the sky then took center stage—bands of orange, mango, citrus yellow,. pink—drenched the horizon in beautiful ribbons while a light blue ocean rolled calmly underneath.

"You see the appeal, right?" Faye whispered in her ear.

"I see the appeal," she said.

They enjoyed their cool drinks and ate Ali's charcuterie art. Blair felt at home, calm. Dare she even say happy? After all that had transpired in just a few whirlwind days.

Operation Good Mom would mean she'd need to be happy. She would try to transfer that feeling to the baby. How? No idea.

She felt at home. Even though there were a million loose ends in every corner of her life. The sky and the sea breeze were like a warm hug, helping her forget that all her problems would be there tomorrow.

She could worry about them then.

Nine

## JOETTA

For the first three days that her big sister was in critical condition, Joetta had to bob and weave. She tried to avoid being there when her three daughters were there. She let Jorge know when she was coming and going. She spent time with her sister while also performing a delicate dance—if she knew one of the girls was going to be there to take a shift, she left at least ten minutes before that shift would start. Joetta wouldn't let anything come between her and her sister, but she wasn't a monster. Jorge didn't need to have family drama play out in the waiting room while Didi was fighting for her actual life.

At Didi's hospital bedside, she had a lot of time to think; too much time, probably. The questions played over and over in her head. The mistakes she'd made were writ large in her mind. The work she'd done to move on, to have a life after Bruce Kelly, seemed to be crumbling.

*What do I owe to the girls? Probably everything.*
*What do I owe to her sister? Certainly everything.*

Giving the girls The Sea Turtle was her way protected them. At first, she thought it would lure them, so they could be a family here.

She'd quickly learned, however, that Bruce wasn't going to let that happen. Not a chance. So, then she'd told herself it was a little nest egg—that property was a tangible way for them to have something of her, even if they didn't know it.

Well, now they knew it.

They knew she was alive. They knew she had abandoned them. And no amount of gifting after the fact was going to earn her forgiveness.

Joetta sat by Didi for a four-hour stretch in the middle of the night. Her shift allowed Jorge to go home. None of them was young, and Jorge was no longer the strong, healthy man he once was. She hoped Jorge would survive Didi's hospitalization. It was a real concern. Didi and Jorge were one person now; could one half live without the other?

The intricate cat-and-mouse game she was playing to avoid the girls at least spared Jorge one more problem.

Joetta was there from midnight until 4 am—well, till 3:50. At 4 am, Blair would come, or Faye, or Ali. They didn't even pass in the hall. Joetta crept around corners and used the stairs so as not to see them in an elevator.

The important thing was making sure that Didi was safe, free of the mess that Joetta had caused.

These days, Joetta didn't sleep much anyway. The older you got, the less you were able to get those luxurious sleep-till-noon days. Most days, something would wake her up at 5 am, even if she hadn't gone to bed till after the late-night talk shows.

But between Joetta and her daughters, Jorge was able to sleep —or at least try to—from midnight to 8 am It was something.

Finally, on the fifth day, they got some good news.

Didi was better. Her bypass surgery had worked. Her heart was beating, and it was strong.

And slowly she was waking up. She wasn't herself yet, but she was no longer unconscious and unable to ask for help. She was also oriented. Didi knew she was in the hospital.

Most importantly, Didi was able to speak for herself, ask for what she needed. No one needed to be there twenty-four hours a day.

In fact, Didi started to insist she get some "me time." That was sweet. Didi was aware that all of them were exhausted.

After five days of constant bedside visits, it was a relief to have Didi awake, and aware, and there. Didi was so aware, she wanted to hear all about the grenade she'd dropped into their ordered existence in the midst of a medical crisis.

Joetta could always talk to Didi about what she'd done. Didi loved her even though Joetta wasn't sure if she deserved any love at all.

"So, you met the girls?" Didi asked her at 3 am. The patient had been awakened by the middle-of-the-night blood draw. Didi's voice was breathy, but her eyes were sharp.

"I did."

"How'd that go?"

"As you might expect."

"They're wonderful, wonderful girls. I've gotten to know them all—well, not so much Blair yet. But Faye and Ali are amazing."

"I would expect that to be true. They were amazing children. And I didn't have a chance to really mess them up."

"Oh, stop, you're all alive, there's always hope." Didi closed her eyes. She was out of the immediate woods, and she'd go from here to a rehab facility if she was lucky. Didi needed sleep, hydration, rehab, and more than anything else, peaceful time to get better.

For now, she was conscious. That was good.

"Ali is the tough one; she knows, she remembers the real me."

"The real you was sick then, but yes, you do have some work to do with that one."

"Do you really think they'll want to hear from me at all, after what I did?"

"I think those three girls will forgive you. And I think those three girls need a mom."

Joetta's breath caught at hearing that. *She was their mother.*

The only way she had survived the last decades, knowing she was their mother, was by trying to forget she was their mother. *What kind of mother could she even claim to be?*

"My advice is start with the little one," Didi said, "She's got no baggage with you."

"My advice is for you to stop worrying about the little drama you started and start worrying about getting better."

"Yeah, yeah, I got it. I just wish they would have done me a solid and given me a tummy tuck while they jump-started my heart. I could get out my old bikini."

The two laughed. It was good to joke and smile a little bit.

Joetta gently hugged her sister and let her fall asleep again. She also got out of there before anyone else arrived. That crisis was averted one more day.

One issue had to be dealt with now; no more avoiding it.

Banks. Her lying had started with him. And she'd done it brilliantly.

As she drove home from the hospital, she tried to put into place what she was going to say to her husband. Joetta would have to tell him something about herself that showed her to be a terrible person. She'd tried to be a good person ever since the moment she married Banks, but it didn't erase what she'd done—that she had left her daughters. It didn't matter that it was forced upon her. She should've fought harder. That's all she could think—she should've fought harder.

As the dawn turned to morning, Joetta sat in the huge kitchen of the five thousand-square-foot home that Banks had built for her after they got married.

She poured some coffee. Banks was not afflicted with sleep

problems. He could always sleep. He could always snore, too, but it was music to her ears. After losing one family, she held tightly to her second chance. For dear life, really.

Since the moment she'd married Banks, she's had a happy ending—tarnished as it may be by her first act, her second act was something she fiercely protected.

By nine in the morning, her husband, Banks, walked into the kitchen and gave her a sweet smile.

"You're back!"

"I am."

"How's your sister?"

"Better. I think my late nights are over."

"Good. I don't like you driving at four in the morning."

"Oh, I'm fine. Traffic is the best it ever gets at four in the morning."

"True."

Banks came over and kissed her cheek. "And you made coffee. That's why I love you."

"*That's* why you love me?"

They smiled. The familiarity that they had developed over the decades was her warm blanket, her rock. The home, the life she'd built—it was a miracle to her. But it was built on a lie. One she still told, almost to the point that it felt like the truth.

Joetta looked at Banks. He loved her. He took care of her. He thought the sun rose and set on her.

"What's on your schedule today, dear?"

"11:30 meeting at the club. Something about a new vendor for our top-shelf liquors. I wanted Troy to deal with it, but alas, he knows how picky I am about the bourbon. And then I've got a one o'clock tee time."

Her beloved husband still managed the golf club and resort. At her insistence, he did now rely on a team of day-to-day hands-on managers—but he still liked to be the boss. As long as Boss Man could have that one o'clock tee time.

The club was their lives. It was his business. It was their social life. It was their charity. It was their community.

She wondered what would happen to that community if they knew what she'd left behind in Ohio. They'd believed her fiction that she'd traveled the world and come home to Florida to settle down.

What she had actually done was have a succession of children, descend into alcoholism, and crash the car while driving with her children.

When she returned to Florida, she'd done it as an unfit mother and in the clutches of her parents. They had been her only source of potential support, the ones who had kicked her out for being pregnant. They didn't ask why she'd returned sans baby. Her worst instincts had come from her own mother, she knew.

The answer to all her problems back then was Banks. He was her savior. That and AA.

She'd never had another drink. It was too risky; she knew where that road had led her before.

When everyone else at the club had their mimosas or Bloody Marys, she had her Shirley Temple and Diet Coke. She never missed alcohol, though sometimes, especially right now, it would be nice to forget, however she could, about what was going on in her life.

The reckoning she'd avoided was upon her.

Should she tell Banks now? Should she let him have his meeting? Should she let him have his tee time before she revealed what a terrible person she was?

She had lied for so long—it would be easy to keep lying.

How could she start? How could he forgive her? Would he walk out? Cut her off?

There was no starting over at her age. Would she be able to hang on to sobriety? She'd been raised with a silver spoon and married a rich man, the second time around. The one period of her life when she'd had to clip coupons and pinch pennies, she'd failed.

And the years had softened her a little. Before, she'd been sure the bad guy in the story was Bruce Kelly.

But now she wondered, was it really all Bruce Kelly's fault? A lot was, but the deep-seated fears and doubts of her own character, abilities, and heart had wormed their way out from her stomach to her brain.

Joetta Bennett Kelly Armstrong was not the princess in the tower, innocent, wronged, cursed. She was just as complicit in her own nightmare as Bruce. She didn't know how to spin the story so that Banks would see her the way he did today. She was the angelic love of his life. She knew she wasn't worthy of that pedestal he had her on. She never was.

The words didn't come. Banks came over and kissed her on the forehead.

"I'll be done early today. Do you want to meet me for a massage after?"

*No. I don't deserve that. No. I deserve to be kicked out.*

She wasn't going to do it. She couldn't do it. The truth was her enemy then and now.

"That's lovely, I'll pop over after my auxiliary meeting."

She was on half a dozen charity committees. She loved her life. She had clawed her way to it.

She knew it was at the expense of her daughters, which made her a terrible person.

"You look like you're a million miles away. What's going on in that beautiful head of yours?"

Banks. He believed her b.s., she flung some more. Like she'd been doing for decades.

"Just thinking about whether we have enough high-ticket items for the charity auction. We're planning on it when the ladies come over."

"Selfless as always." Banks kissed her on the lips this time. She kissed him back. He smiled and put his coffee mug on the counter.

"Aviva! Mrs. Armstrong is on her own in the kitchen. Just

warning you, so she doesn't get any ideas that she should be cooking."

It was a family joke; how bad she was at cooking. Aviva was their maid and cook.

"Don't worry, Mr. A. I've got it."

Aviva took the mug and put it in the dishwasher.

"I've pressed the pink sweater set for your meeting later. Is that still what you'd like to wear?"

"Thank you, yes, Aviva."

Joetta's husband left her in good hands; Aviva fussed around the kitchen doing the things Joetta didn't want to do.

"I'm going to lie down for a little nap, wake me before noon, please."

"Yes, ma'am."

Joetta would keep lying; she'd do it to keep what she had. But also, she was greedy. She wanted her girls, too. Somehow, she'd find a way to have it all without losing a thing.

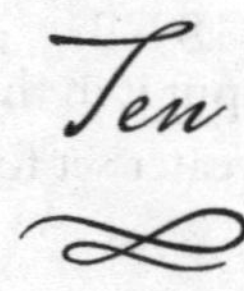

# Ten

## FAYE

Faye left Ali to her tasks. The list was long, and they wanted to help, but as Faye knew, Ali didn't do therapy or counseling: she did tasks. Endless tasks.

Faye worried that there would be a reckoning for Ali, for the emotions she'd suppressed in the name of efficiency and family duty.

Ali was Ali, and Faye knew that any love and nurturing they had growing up was from Ali. Not Joetta. Still. The thoughts of their mother, out there, what could be, what they need to talk about, were hard to suppress.

Faye would have to take a page out of Ali's book. Keep busy or drown in "what could be."

Faye and Blair knew that Ali could manage almost anything she put her mind to. That was a rule they lived by; kind of like the rule that you left Dad alone when he was in the garage fixing something.

Finding a way to keep busy was now on Faye's priority list.

46

Step one? Find a job that didn't depend on The Sea Turtle's bookings.

Jorge was with Didi at the hospital, and Sawyer was at the pottery studio. Even her baby sister—who she'd helped grow up and get out of Ohio—wanted some time to nap and assess her own future. Which was fair.

For the first time in a while, Faye didn't have a bunch of people to manage.

She decided to do her favorite thing: dig in the dirt.

If Ali's therapy was massive undertakings like conventions and hotel renovations, Faye's was gardening. Dirty overalls, clear mind.

Faye spent her first official morning as a Florida resident pulling weeds along the parking lot of The Sea Turtle. She wasn't quite satisfied with the look of the landscaping that led up to each of the cottages. She needed some edging—maybe—to keep things looking intentional. But also wild, sure. *Wild on purpose? Was that a thing?*

Garden design aesthetic aside, it would be easier for them to assess each cottage's maintenance needs if they weren't overgrown with plants and weeds.

Faye got out her app for plant ID and identified three different plants that were crowding the Strawberry Cottage. But she also had to assess whether they were allowed to be pulled. She found out that several different species along the beach were protected.

After a couple of hours of clean-up, she moved from that task to the pool.

The pool had gone through a massive transformation. She was really proud of Sawyer for the work he'd done. The water was crystal blue, clear as can be, and the formerly broken ceramic tiles were either repaired or replaced. Thanks to Sawyer's new hobby— scratch that, it wasn't Sawyer's *hobby* right now. Sawyer had plans to become a ceramic tile artist as a *job*.

She shook her head. Well, she guessed that if that didn't work out, there were plenty of pools he could help clean.

She still wasn't sure that "ceramic tile artist" was going to put food on the table. He was in his twenties, though, and putting food on the table wasn't something he was all that worried about. Mooching food off *her* plate would be the backup she predicted.

Sawyer was talented, but wasn't it just like her with the flowers? It was a hobby, not a jobby.

Faye put her worries aside one by one as she deadheaded flowers along the pool. She adjusted the pots they'd planted and realized maybe some could be cut for a bouquet.

"There are plenty of you; I think Didi's room could use a pick-me-up." Yes, she was talking to the plants. This was much easier than talking to humans.

Faye went about selecting a few hibiscus blooms, lantana, and coral bells for a lovely little bouquet for the hospital. She had a fist full of flowers that looked raucous and wild but also cohesive.

The colors, textures, and heights moved to the front of her mind, and her worries about family drama settled back.

Now, to find a vase—or, as the fancy décor shows, called it—a vessel. Faye wandered to the office building for The Sea Turtle to see if they had any options. Or maybe she'd need a trip to the thrift store for a vase. *Ugh. Vessel. Heck with it.* Faye would always call it a vase, especially since she'd arranged her first bouquet in a coffee can.

# *Eleven*

**1983**
Faye

She started out with the dandelion. She knew what the dandelion was, but they weren't enough. She looked at her Dixie cup and realized that wasn't enough either. She toddled back into the house and found a big jelly jar, dumped the jelly into the sink, and took it outside.

Her whole focus was on filling that jar with flowers. The dandelions were in a just-in-case flower. They weren't pretty enough. They weren't flowery enough.

She walked over to the flower bed on the side of the house. There were flowers she didn't know the names of—but she knew the names of some of them. There were snapdragons. She liked the name of that. She picked a few of the snapdragons. They were tall. Pink. She liked the way the jelly jar was starting to look, tall floppies, short cuties, yellow and pink mixing together. Faye smiled at her creation.

She moved on. It wasn't done.

The jar needed to look like a waterfall. Her little fingers reached out to pull some flowers from next door and put those in the jar.

"Now it's looking good," she said out loud.

She continued. She realized she needed to make more than one bouquet. Now that she had this one looking better, she'd make another.

She went into her daddy's workshop. He had jars and jars and jars. She used the stepstool. She climbed up on it, and she took one of the jars that only had a few rusty nails in it. She dumped the rusty nails onto a pile.

This. This is better.

It was a coffee can. She would fill that coffee can with a bunch of other flowers.

Weeping willow. She knew what that was. She used her hands to climb the tree and pull down some weeping willow branches. She put those in the coffee can.

She spent the whole afternoon in the warmth of the sun, skipping around the garden, looking for different things to put in different jars. Time flew by like the bees and the butterflies. She knew they were all good for the flowers; most of her friends screamed if they saw a bee. So silly.

At six o'clock, it all went wrong.

Daddy came home.

First, she heard him in the kitchen. He was moving things around. Picking things up and putting them down, with a crashing sound.

She sneaked into the house and up the stairs with one of her special creations. She put it on the nightstand for Mommy.

Mommy was sleeping.

"Mommy?"

Mommy tried to answer.

Oh no. All she could think was: *If she could just show Daddy all the flowers that she put in the jelly jar, he would be happy, and*

*Mommy wouldn't be in trouble. She didn't want to get in trouble. She'd bring Mommy all her bouquets.*

She ran back outside to the picnic table where she had filled at least six different jars and cans with flowers from their entire yard.

She would show all of these flowers to Daddy and Mommy! That would be perfect!

"Come outside and see! Come look!"

He didn't hear.

She ran in again with her little plan. This time, she'd tell Daddy what she'd done, and he could see her pretty flowers.

Her daddy was opening the refrigerator.

"No groceries—big surprise." He closed the refrigerator hard. Glasses clinked inside the door as it slammed.

"Daddy! Come see what I did!"

"What are you talking about? Where's your mother?"

At that moment, Mommy woke up and came down.

Mommy walked into the kitchen.

She was wearing a red halter top tied at the neck and the waist, and a pair of white shorts. She looked like a movie star.

"Have you been sleeping?"

"Oh, Bruce, what are you yelling about?"

"Do you see this mess in the sink? What a disaster!"

"Mommy! Daddy! Come look what I made!"

She said it about three times until finally Bruce had to go outside.

"Doesn't anyone in this family know how to work a broom for all this mess in here?"

"Daddy, come look," Faye said again.

"Fine. What do you want to show me?"

She looked behind her. Her daddy and mommy—for a moment—weren't fighting. They were following her to her masterpiece of floral brilliance.

"Look what I made!"

Coffee cans. Jelly jars. Dixie cups. Everything she could get her hands on, filled with every kind of flower she could pick.

Her mommy clapped.

"Oh, Faye, you are brilliant. This is so magical."

She jumped up and down. Oh, Mommy loved it. She *knew* Mommy would love it.

She looked at Mommy.

Daddy looked at Mommy.

"She threw out a perfectly good jar of jelly. Is that the can of—where did you put the screws that I had in that coffee can?"

He continued to look at all her projects.

"Where—did you use the flowers from the flower beds to make these? That's landscaping. We're going to look like the worst house on the block again."

Daddy wagged his finger at her and got close to her face.

"Faye Kelly, this is a waste of money and time. You made a mess of our landscaping, and you made a mess of my workshop—not to mention the kitchen sink. You're gonna help me clean this up."

Faye started to cry.

"Bruce, leave her alone. I'll clean it up."

Mommy stepped between her and Daddy. She picked Faye up.

Faye couldn't see anymore. She was crying so much. She buried her head in Mommy's shoulder.

"Daddy didn't like the flowers," she hiccupped. "Daddy doesn't like the flowers. Daddy is mad at me."

Mommy stroked her hair.

"I *love* the flowers. They are beautiful, and you are so talented. I wouldn't know how to put those flowers in those jars just that way. Each one of them is a work of art, my sweet girl. Little flower girl."

Faye never picked flowers from their yard again. She didn't want Daddy to yell at her.

But she also never forgot how happy those flowers had made Mommy.

# Twelve

**PRESENT DAY**
Ali

The news on Didi's health was all good. Things were going in the right direction for her aunt. She didn't know if she was ready to call Didi her aunt.

*What was the cliché? What did Didi know and when did she know it?*

Her Aunt Didi had lied just like Joetta had. So many lies.

Ali's husband had lied; that's what ended their marriage. Her father had lied; that's what made this place a mystery their entire lives.

Joetta had lied, left them, and lied; that's what turned Ali into a de facto mother to her baby sisters. That was what forced a child into a role that was all responsibility.

Ali felt bruised. If she unpacked the scope of what Didi and Joetta and Bruce had made up, of the crap they'd dished out, she'd walk out onto the beach and dig a hole in the sand and climb in. What kind of person did this? Much less a whole family

54

of people, conspiring against their kids. It made her sick to her stomach.

Ali held onto the fact that her sisters weren't lying. They were the victims, like she'd been. They were the only ones whom she trusted right now. And maybe forever.

Only a few weeks ago, Ali would have been the point person on Didi's health with Jorge until their kids arrived. She wouldn't have thought twice about doing everything she could to be by Didi's bedside.

Now, there was just so much baggage.

Didi had Jorge and Joetta. The Kelly Sisters filled in the gaps until they could figure out where their aunt fit into their lives. Ali was sure their mother did not fit in and never would.

There was another person who gave her hope, Jorge.

Jorge wasn't at full strength after all his medical issues but insisted on being with his wife. His sun, moon, and stars were Didi.

Ali had loved Didi, too, and trusted her, until all this hit the fan. Now, Didi just needed their help, and Jorge their support. So that was it. The Kelly Sisters were there for Didi and Jorge, and God help Joetta if she tried any of her b.s.

Which left Ali back at The Sea Turtle. This was a project she could manage. The place needed her, and everything about it was concrete. It may need money and elbow grease and a million other things, but it wasn't mysterious. It was real.

However it came to be that Joetta had arranged for the Kelly Sisters to have this property, they had it. She had it, and she was going to make it work.

Which today, meant meeting with an inspector about the Inn. The beach homes were manageable. Sure, they needed updates, but the updates were plumbing, roofing, and then the fun part, decorating. Her daughter, Katie, was helping her with décor decisions via FaceTime. They decided each of the beach houses would have with its own little beach vibe. The Key Lime and the Blueberry Bungalow were in the best shape. That left the Lemon Love Shack, the Strawberry Hideaway, the Pink Lady, and the Mango Mansion on her list for upgrades. Daunting but not impossible.

The less fun and downright terrifying part was the hotel. It had six rooms and a penthouse on the top; it required repair and maintenance on a level Ali hadn't managed before without a building staff! And thanks to Ted's attempt to sabotage her, inspectors were on the way to the Inn. Recent tragedies and weather events meant the safety of condos and hotels was top of mind for the state. Safety was also at the top of Ali's mind, but it would have been nice to have had a little time before officials showed up. No such luck, thanks to Ted.

Two weeks after Ted had left and one week since Didi's massive health issue, two inspectors were set to arrive to go through the Inn from top to bottom.

Worrying about that inspection had given her several sleepless nights already, along with her totally bonkers family.

Two inspectors arrived, and she greeted them with a bright smile. It was time to take her medicine and figure out what she really was up against with the Inn.

Ali had done all she could to be sure the obvious things at the hotel were fixed. She knew they'd see that the roof needed repair, that there were several issues with plumbing, and that the electrical system was thirty years old. But all of that was manageable. Ali believed she had it under control.

The inspections of hotels and condos were called milestone structural inspections, she'd learned, and it was as serious as it got.

After being alerted to the need for it by the county via Ted, she quickly became an expert on what the experts would look at. Henry, who'd owned a business in Haven Beach for years, helped her find reputable inspectors. Aside from being the best thing in her life these days, Henry was also trying to help her not stop her from succeeding.

This was important because she'd also learned she didn't have much time; owners were obligated to get the inspections two weeks after ownership. She was late, but hopefully wouldn't get penalized.

Ali was trying to build an oasis for people. She wanted them to feel like she did, at home and at ease on this gorgeous beach. Which meant facing the music on the stuff that Didi and Jorge had neglected in their old age.

The inspection team looked nice enough; she took that as a good omen. Eric Chase and Paul Gomez were partners in CGA Architectural Engineering. And Henry had said they were regular customers since the day he took over his restaurant.

They arrived in a logoed pick-up truck. They both wore CGA-branded dress shirts.

"Ali, hi, I'm Eric, and this is Paul."

"Great to meet you both, I appreciate you fitting this in."

"Henry said you were under the gun on time, we get it," said Eric.

"I am, yes. I'm new to all of it in this state, just trying not to get shut down."

"This place is a gem, wow! A throwback for sure, not many buildings left from the war era," Paul said as he put a hand over his brow to shield his eyes from the sun.

Ali looked up and down the three-story structure that was now hers and her sisters to deal with. "It does feel vintage, and I do have a lot of work to do to make it ready for guests, so just ignore the décor," Ali said. She was nervous, no question.

"We care about the big things, the structural things; we need to be sure you can sleep soundly at night and so can your guests," Eric said. He had a warm smile, and it soothed her nerves a bit. But only a bit.

"Let me be honest, I didn't get this place after an inspection; I didn't buy it. I inherited it...well, was given it, whatever...the point is, there could be surprises."

"There are always surprises, but when we're done, you'll have the facts. That's better than not knowing when the other shoe is going to flop," Paul said.

"What?"

"The other shoe is going to drop, not flop," Eric laughed. "Paul is famous for mangling expressions."

"Why would shoes drop? They flop? Like a flip-flop, right?" Paul looked at her with this serious inquiry.

"I guess," Ali said, and Eric shook his head.

"We'll get started. You can just make sure everything is unlocked and let us go to town, or you can come along, whatever you'd like. But it is going to take several hours, and it's already in the mid-'80s."

"Will you show me what you find, walk me through, so I can manage a cottage check-in?"

"Of course, we've got your cell, right?"

"Right."

"Okay, we're gonna get going, we'll text you if we run into any issues with access or with questions. Or if any shoes seem floppy."

Ali smiled at Paul, making fun of himself. She got good vibes from these two. She would have to thank Henry yet again. He never steered her wrong.

While Eric and Paul headed to the hotel, Ali found Sawyer setting the beach up for the new guests. A young couple on their honeymoon had booked the Key Lime cottage, and they were set to arrive any second.

Sawyer, Faye's son, was her go-to lately, with Jorge out of the loop, taking care of Didi. But she knew it wasn't a permanent situation. Jorge would be back, and she knew Sawyer was soon to be very busy with his ceramics coursework. Faye wasn't sold on Sawyer's plan, but Ali got to be the fun aunt in this scenario. Likely, she'd be just as worried about his career path if he were her kid, but it wasn't her role.

Faye's fears that a person couldn't support themselves making pottery were legitimate worries. But the worries were piling up, and Ali was all stocked on that front. If her nephew wanted to throw clay, and it made him happy, that was fine for her.

"Those the engineer guys?" Sawyer unfurled the canvas of the beach cabanas they had set up along their section of beach. His blonde hair flopped in the wind, and he was constantly pushing it from one side to the other.

"Yep, cross your fingers on that," she said.

"For sure. What time for the love birds?"

"They said 11 am, so I'm doing a once-over at the Key Lime. If you could just make sure the pool looks shipshape, we're good."

"Will do!"

Sawyer had done so much to make the pool look amazing. He'd recreated vintage tiles and replaced the cracked ones. *Maybe his career path will be okay?*

She left him to his work. Ali took a beat; she looked out at the beach. Her mother's reappearance had shaken everything she believed about her past, her own history. And now the actual ground she was responsible for managing might very well be shaky too.

The water was rougher today than yesterday; the waves crashed into the sand more than the gentle rolling she'd first experienced when she arrived only a few short months ago.

Ali didn't have time to kick off her shoes and sink her toes in. Instead, she had to dig in her heels and do what she did best. Manage multiple crises at a time.

That was where she was really at home.

* * *

Their inspection took a couple of hours. Ali, in that time, checked in her newlywed couple—Van and Carrie Connors.

Meeting them took her mind back to when she was that young and newly married.

Ted had planned the honeymoon. They'd gone to the battlefields of the Civil War. Not exactly romantic, but then again, he was a history professor.

As they toured the battlefields, he took notes and mused in detail about how this or that would make it into his epic historical work on whatever the heck.

She believed him, back then, that he'd be the next David McCollough. She was very young and naïve. Ted wrote a few papers, enough to get tenure. But no novel, no big vision, just big talk.

These kids who checked in, though, were sweet. Van and Carrie seemed to be on the same page: a honeymoon in the Key Lime with the sound of the ocean waves, on a budget—there were worse ways to start a marriage.

Ali made sure to stock the refrigerator with some champagne and a few other essentials. She didn't always do that—because with kids and families, everyone had their own favorites—but with these two, she hoped they were way too busy to think about groceries. After she gave them the tour and got them settled, she went back to the hotel in search of the inspectors.

They were in the lower units—pointing, talking, writing things down. They asked a couple of questions, questions she wished Jorge were here to answer, but she did her best. She felt guilty that she didn't know more about the building and explained —probably too many times—that she hadn't bought it; she inherited it.

She hoped Jorge had done enough over the years. She left him out of it, though; he had to worry about Didi.

"Well," one of the inspectors said, "we're pretty good here— the inspection, I mean. Well, let's just say we're done."

Eric and Paul had been all smiles and upbeat when they'd met but now had gotten very serious. Ali could read their faces: all wasn't well with the hotel.

"Now, we can give you our preliminary thoughts. This isn't

the final inspection report—got some data to calculate, that kind of thing."

"I understand, just a ballpark of what I'm in for."

Eric took off his eyeglasses and looked at her, not the clipboard that likely contained a list that was a mile long.

"Here's the thing. There are some small things to be taken care of. You know about the roof, you know your plumbing systems, and at least half the units are probably not up to code anymore. But that's not the biggest problem."

"What's the biggest problem—I mean, to me, plumbing and roofing seem big?"

The inspectors looked at each other. "Again, this is preliminary—you're going to need a better survey of what we're about to tell you—but...you've got foundation issues."

"Foundation issues?"

"Yeah. That's why we're doing these inspections. You know all about that condo collapse. Well, here in Florida, things are wet. This is sand, it's rough, and some things need to be done now with the new regs to bolster foundations that didn't used to have to be done."

*Did that mean Jorge wasn't up to speed on what needed to be done?* That tracked in Ali's mind, based on the fact that he could barely walk when she first met him.

"I can see why some of these things were neglected...but if you're going to get approval to open this hotel to guests, you're going to have to fix some foundational structural issues."

"OK—yeah, of course we want to be safe. Do you know how much that costs?"

"Well, you know—we're here to assess. We're not trying to sell you. We can just tell you what needs to be done."

"But you have to have some idea. What am I looking at here—ten thousand? Twenty thousand?"

"Well, I think that's kind of low," Eric said.

Ali's throat went dry, she tried to swallow, and her own spit felt foreign, she didn't need this on top of all the other things going on. But here it was.

She threw out another number. "Hundred thousand?" Ali stopped outbidding herself on the job. They didn't answer.

She pushed.

"Is this a *million-dollar* repair?"

The two inspectors seemed nice. They didn't want to tell her, but they also didn't seem to want to lie.

"It could be...it could be."

Ali put her head in her hands. She knew the land, at one point, was worth quite a bit of money—not the structures themselves, but the land. Had she made a huge financial mistake? Just like Ted said she had.

All of a sudden, the idea of making The Sea Turtle Cottages and Resort a profitable enterprise seemed like a dumb idea—if not impossible.

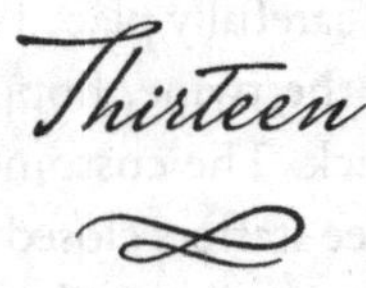

# Thirteen

## FAYE

Every time Faye stepped into The Mangrove Garden Grotto, she was in awe. It was the Disneyland of greenhouses and nurseries, she decided.

She didn't know exactly what she was after—but a job would be nice. Maybe Rudy Palmer would know of something, although she didn't know what she was qualified for. She'd worked at the auto plant for decades, and the skill set she had...well, she didn't know what it translated to in any other setting.

Certainly, Rudy didn't need her to manage a crew of thirty, make sure they had breaks, make sure they were covered if someone was sick, and a million other things that union reps like herself had to deal with. But still—she didn't know many people here in Haven Beach, and any reason to come to the greenhouse was a good reason, in her opinion.

She found Rudy in the parking lot, loading a tree. She tried not to notice how good he looked. She was not in the market for a man; she was in the market for a job.

"Hand me the twine," Rudy told a young employee wearing a Mangrove Grotto t-shirt. Two others stood back, looking slightly stressed out. More stressed than a greenhouse ought to make a person, Faye thought.

She watched as Rudy carefully placed the tree in the back of the truck, tied it down with the twine, hopped out, and then lightly tapped the side of the truck. The customer gave him a thumbs-up and drove off. Rudy's three staffers closed in on the boss.

"So, you're saying we don't have anyone to do that arrangement?"

"Well, I can do it, but she isn't very happy, this bride. And I've never done a full wedding, or really any event."

"Fine. Well, get started on the notes of what they wanted, and we'll just hope for the best. I'll call Babs and try to guilt her into it. It really is unacceptable."

His employees slowly sauntered off to complete the tasks at hand. The situation seemed urgent, but the staff seemed reluctant. Faye decided this wasn't the best time, but what the heck, she was here. She stepped forward and piped up.

"So...you do weddings?" she asked.

"Well, *I* don't do weddings." The furrow in Rudy's brow smoothed as he smiled at her.

*Wow, okay, that's a great smile.* She'd been trying to put that out of her mind. *Focus, Faye, focus.*

"I thought you were gone."

"Yeah. I'm back."

His smile erupted, and it made her feel some type of way, as Sawyer said, to see his reaction.

"Yeah. I'm back."

"That's the best news I've had all day. All week. Heck, possibly all year long."

"Well, I think I'm gonna be here a while. I'm gonna sell my house back in Toledo."

"Wow. You're gonna turn into a Floridian, like the rest of us?" Rudy's tan arms made her realize just how Florida he was.

"I realized there was no reason for me to deal with February in Toledo ever again, as long as we had The Sea Turtle."

"That's logical."

"It sounds like you have a situation." She wanted to get to the issue at hand, not flirting, which she was doing, inadvertently. Apparently, handsome men with green thumbs and tan arms were all it took for her to turn into Scarlet O'Hara.

"Oh yeah. No, I provide the flowers to a couple of floral designers. And unfortunately, a particular floral designer has made all kinds of promises to a local bride and is—well—sick as a dog. And she's thrown the ball back to *us*. We've already got all the flowers in the house, and no one to arrange them. I really don't want this to be my problem, but of course, it is."

"I mean, the three staffers there ought to be able to handle it, right?"

"No, they're the growers—like me. I mean, I *love* flowers, plants, trees, shrubbery, all of it, but in the dirt, not in the vase or a bouquet. I do not have the flower arranging gene."

"Oh, come on. This place *is* your bouquet."

And she wasn't lying. The Grotto was a work of floral art in Faye's estimation. Trays of flowers were everywhere, along with all of the greenhouse staples. Rudy seemed to be studying her, and her face started to get uncomfortably red.

"You wouldn't mind—I don't know—taking a look at what they're doing back there?"

"Well, I'm not a floral designer either. But I can...I mean, I have made a few arrangements."

Faye was downplaying her skill set when it came to making vases and floral displays. She actually loved doing it. She'd been doing it before she could even read. But she was not a floral designer by any stretch of the imagination. No one paid her to do it. She had no training, just a passion for her hobby. It was hardly something to put on a resume.

"Just look it over, give your two cents, last I heard you were retired, right?"

"Right."

"So, you've got a few minutes. Let me take you back to my guys. They've got the list that the bride ordered. You could at least see if they're on the right track."

"Okay." Against her better judgment, she wanted to help Rudy; she wanted to spend time here, she'd sought him out after all.

"And listen—I'd pay you. You're saving my behind."

Her blush threatened to come back.

"I *am* looking for a job."

"I'll pay the going rate for a floral designer."

"I thought I was saving your butt; the price just went up," she said.

Rudy laughed and then put his hand out to guide her to the workroom.

There, they found Rudy's staff arguing and reading a sheet of paper and doing very little floral arranging. They stared at the scissors and floral tape and seemed to be unsure what to do next.

She had to have at least as much experience as these three, who looked to be around Sawyer's age. At the very least, she knew how to manage people.

Faye was determined to do her best to get Rudy Palmer right with the mother of the bride.

Heck, at the very least, she'd earn a few bucks.

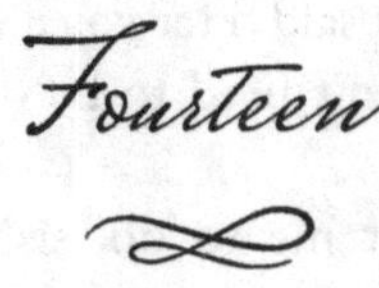

# Fourteen

## JOETTA

Joetta was feeling better—at least about one aspect of her life. Didi was about to be transferred to an extended care facility so she could rehab and get stronger before she went home. She had a long way to go, but every day she was getting stronger.

She wasn't dying. Not on Joetta's watch, no way.

Joetta helped Didi pack up the cards and flowers that had accumulated in her room before Jorge's arrival for the transfer to the step-down facility.

For the first time, Didi was strong enough to bring up what Joetta did not want to talk about. The girls.

"So...have you had any contact with the girls?" Didi asked.

"No. Ali has made it clear. They don't want that."

"What do *you* want?"

"I just want to not rock the boat."

"That doesn't sound like my sister."

"I know. But I don't have any rights. I don't have any reason to think they would ever forgive me."

"I think you might be surprised," she said. "These three girls are amazing."

"I know. No fault of mine. Hate to say it, but maybe Bruce Kelly did a good job. They did better without me."

"Oh, come on," Didi said. Her voice was still weak, reminding Joetta that her sister didn't need to be dealing with family stress right now.

"What do you want me to do, sis? We're supposed to be keeping you calm."

"I'm fine."

But she didn't look fine. She looked a lot better, but she still was weak. It scared Joetta to think that Didi wasn't strong, indestructible, eternal.

She stopped—or tried to stop—this line of discussion. It only led to stress on everybody's part.

"Look, it may take time, but I bet they'll come around."

"So how do I make that happen? Show up on all family holidays with potato salad and apologies? I don't think so."

"Maybe, a covered dish does wonders, you know."

"Big sis, let's just focus on *you*, OK? You scared the crap out of Jorge."

"I know. He's been great, though."

"Of course he has. Did you tell Banks?"

That was a conversation decades in the making, one Didi had nagged about over the years. Joetta had ignored her, had avoided the subject, and had lied through her teeth.

"How'd that go?"

"Well, Banks was...OK. No problem. He loved the idea. Not gonna leave me. We're good."

"You didn't tell him. Got it. And he's never gonna leave you. You know that."

"You think? I think when all this comes to light, it's going to ruin him."

As she finished saying it, she looked over at Didi for some sort of guidance or response.

Didi was asleep.

*So much the better,* thought Joetta. *She needs her rest.*

Her best bet now was to try to be a good sister. Try to be a good wife. Try to be a good mother to all her daughters. Even if that meant staying out of their way.

Didi had an optimism that Joetta didn't share. Joetta was just trying to keep the lies intact, the ones she'd carefully constructed for survival.

She pulled the cover up around her sister, now totally out. Joetta quietly left the hospital room; Jorge would be there within the hour. He, too, would let Didi sleep and likely snooze in the hospital chair next to her.

But Didi's conversation was still in her mind as she walked out of the elevator into the lobby of the hospital.

There she ran—almost practically straight into—Blair.

Blair protectively put her hands over her abdomen. And then her eyes flew wide open.

That's when Joetta realized Blair was pregnant.

"Well...hello."

"Hello."

"Asleep," Joetta pointed up to indicate Didi's room.

"Oh. I'm not headed there."

"No?"

"Oh—I'm sorry."

"OK. I'll get out of your way."

"No, I just...I just want you to know that I'm not the same as Ali."

"What does that mean?"

"It means...maybe we can get coffee."

Joetta could barely believe her ears.

"That would be amazing. You name the time."

"You might need to name the place, too. I'm new to Haven Beach," smiled Blair.

She really was a combination of her and Bruce. Ali was like looking in a mirror—a younger version of her. Faye was Bruce. But Blair...she was the mix. Bruce's dark hair and her blond had been mixed together to form the auburn waves that framed Blair's lovely face. Her eyes, too, were an amber mix of colors.

In Joetta's estimation, Blair got the best of all worlds. And maybe because of it, she was willing to forgive? Is that what she was offering her long-lost mother?

Or maybe it was because she didn't have anything to forget.

It pierced Joetta's heart anytime she thought of the baby she'd left behind—but she also thought of the baby that could've died, thanks to her alcoholism, if she'd stayed.

Didi said she might be surprised by these girls. And maybe, just maybe, even a relationship with *one* was better than nothing.

Joetta walked out of the hospital with two reasons to feel just slightly optimistic.

With Blair...maybe there was some hope.

# Fifteen

## FAYE

Faye walked into the back room to find Rudy's three employees looking at her as though she had the answers. She decided to pretend she did.

"Well, what's the plan?" one finally asked.

"Your name is...?"

"I'm Kyle," said the skinny, tall, and somehow hopeless-looking staffer. He literally looked like he might be drowning.

"And you are?" Faye said to the young woman next to him—looked slightly less afraid, but similarly underwater.

"I'm Marissa. This is Jordan." Marissa pointed to a kid who was carrying flowers stacked up to his chin.

"Hi Marissa. Hi Kyle. Hi Jordan!"

Jordan nodded from behind the blooms.

"I hear you had a floral designer," Faye said.

Kyle shook his head, a vehement no.

Marissa explained the situation.

"Well, Rudy doesn't have a floral arrangement person. He supplies flowers for several different designers. This particular designer is supposed to do a wedding…in about five hours."

This was the first time she'd heard a timetable. Five *hours*? It was midday, on a Friday. *How in the world?*

"Five hours? What happened?"

"Well…she's had an allergic reaction to shellfish, is what we heard."

"So why is this *your* problem? She's going to ruin her reputation, not yours."

Rudy rejoined them after dealing with a customer in the greenhouse.

"It isn't really our problem. Except for—we just felt like we didn't want this poor bride to have nothing."

Faye could imagine the heartbreak of today's bride who meticulously Pinterest-planned everything to be stuck with zero flowers for the big day.

And then Marissa spoke up.

"And if she doesn't have flowers, well…the floral designer's career is over. That would be terrible. She's a nice person, just bad luck. But she'll be hard-pressed to book again if this gets on Yelp or TikTok."

That part was true. Faye knew gigs like photography or floral design, or even small cottage rentals on the beach, depended on good word of mouth and great online reviews. Faye didn't know any other way to start but to just dive in.

"OK, so do we have some idea what she wants?" Faye asked.

"That's the other problem," Kyle said. "We don't."

Marissa stepped in again. "So, the floral designer is actually in the hospital. All of the stuff is on her phone. She put an order in for things but never confirmed—so we don't really know what the bride wants."

"We have a location and the time. Do we know how many bridesmaids? Do we know what else the order entails?"

Marissa went to her computer and pulled up the last email she had from the floral designer.

"One bride, yay, and we have four bridesmaids. Four grooms-men. A groom. It doesn't say here, but I'd also assume we've got parents of the two, and honestly, we should assume four parents on each side."

"That's a lot of parents," Jordan said, though his volume was muffled as he hadn't moved from his spot underneath the flowers.

"Put the flowers down, and we got to plan for a divorce, step-parents, or a grandparent, just in case."

"That's smart," Rudy said.

Faye combed through the email looking for what she could extrapolate. Quantities but not colors!

"Thanks, and this is on the beach, and they have a tent too. We're supposed to do flowers for the head table and flowers for... looks like twenty-five round tables."

At this point, Faye imagined she was starting to look like Kyle, like she might be drowning.

Nope. If she wanted to help here, she had to project confidence. Her flowers were better than no flowers, so she put her shoulders back. Faye had a hair scrunchy on her wrist. She gathered her dark hair in her fist and wound the scrunchy around the pony-tail. It was time to get to work.

She had an idea of quantity, but style? That was going to be the real trick.

"We have no idea what they want as far as the look of this thing, then?"

No one answered.

"OK. OK." Faye racked her brain. She looked at the invoice Rudy produced. The list of flowers could give some clues, but it wasn't enough. She paced back and forth for a moment while the rest of the staff of the Grotto waited for her pronouncement, like she was choosing a new pope.

How could they figure out how to get the bride the wedding of her dreams, make sure the floral designer wasn't ruined for floral design for the rest of her life, and Rudy's business didn't get besmirched in the wake of a disaster?

*A disaster.*

"OK. I've got it. I've got it. What's the bride's name again?"

Marissa gave her the pertinent information, and then Faye pulled up Pinterest on her phone.

After a quick search, and she found it. *Finally, a bit of luck!*

"Ha! Ha!"

She showed her phone to Marissa.

"Does this look like the bride?"

"I've never met her, but...that's the right spelling."

"Facebook," Kyle offered.

"Nope, this is her Pinterest board for weddings. If we assume that these are the floral arrangements she liked—and this is what she shared with the designer—we can at least approximate something. It looks like her colors are peach and blush."

She looked around the room.

The colors that the bride asked for weren't well represented in the number of flowers in the room. She made some mental calculations.

"OK. Let's assume peach is her color. What do we have that's peach? Rudy?"

"I'll go out and see what we've got, peach? And uh, blush?"

"Yep, hang on."

Faye wrote a list of flowers she thought could work, and her brain started envisioning an outdoor wedding. Twenty-five tables. Four groomsmen. Four bridesmaids. Bride. Groom.

"All right, let's work on the main bride's bouquet first. That's what most people are going to notice. Then we'll do the bridesmaids—because if anyone's gonna complain, it's gonna be the bridesmaids. Then we'll work on the tables. Tables first—twenty-five centerpieces next."

Faye's shop steward experience kicked in. It always rode side-by-side next to her fantasies as a floral designer.

Rudy came back with several of the things on her list and asked her to clarify a few more.

But at that point, they were off to the races.

## ALI

Ali looked at the sheet. Some of it she understood; some of it she didn't. What was clear was that her dream was getting more and more expensive.

Bolstering foundation posts underneath the hotel was the big-ticket item. But that wasn't the only problem. There was also the need for a new roof.

There was also a need for new plumbing.

There was also a need for updated signage at all the exits.

There was also a need. And a need. And a need.

She sat in the little office poring over each line.

The engineers said the foundational issue was the one that would prohibit them from getting approval for opening the Inn.

They told her they would bid on the job but also gave her a few other companies. Though honestly, if she could afford this, it would be with them. They seemed reputable and honest, just not cheap. None of it was cheap.

They estimated several hundreds of thousands of dollars to get the Inn up to code. Where would she find that kind of capital, and if she didn't, how that would impact each one of the people that depended on her?

She thought about Faye. Faye had moved here based on Ali's dream. She said she wanted to find a job down here, but what if she didn't? Ali wanted them to live on the rental income from The Sea Turtle. That seemed utterly impossible right now.

Ali hoped that Faye's pension gave her enough leeway to live. Ali squeezed her eyes shut for a second. She imagined having to tell Faye, "Oops, just kidding, we're not making a go of this."

No matter what, it was very clear that there was no way they could afford to keep employees. She'd paid Didi and Jorge; there was zero money for that. She now worried about the older couples' pension. Was it enough? Did they have savings?

Based on the old jewels and clothes that Ali had found of Joetta's, the sisters had pieced together that there was money, somewhere, at some point.

But today? Ali stopped thinking about the older generation. That path led her to Joetta, and she didn't have time for that; Joetta wasn't going to save her. She never had.

But she did need to think about Sawyer. She opened her spreadsheets to look at what she was paying Sawyer. Sawyer had also moved here.

He, too, was going to have to pick up more work as a pool cleaner with Silvio, or as an intern with his school—his school... could Faye afford his school on her retirement and zero hotel income? Columns of numbers scrolled in front of her eyes; each number attached to the dreams and futures of her dearest family.

And then there was Blair—the biggest concern. Her sister was pregnant. She didn't want Blair to work. She didn't want Blair to worry.

She also didn't want Blair to miss a doctor's appointment, which was where her baby sister was right now, at the doctor's.

Ali needed to take on more here. Jorge and Didi needed to retire. That was certain.

Could she do this all by herself? That was the question.

The answer was...she would have to.

The list was long. From light bulbs to walkways to plumbing, the Inn was in need of work.

She'd have to come up with a massive amount of money.

Right now, it looked like a million-dollar problem.

Ali read and re-read the reports from the engineering firm.

She called contractors, she did internet research, and she even phoned her old building foreman at the convention center. All in an attempt to crunch numbers.

Six figures, at least, high six figures. She'd have to come up with nearly a million bucks if they were to save the hotel portion of The Sea Turtle and get it up to code.

Ali sank into the folding chair in The Sea Turtle office.

She looked around the management office-slash-supply closet-slash-laundry facility for the hotel and cottages. As though there would be answers on the metal shelving.

*What was it the kids say? The math wasn't mathing.*

In another two weeks, five of the six cottages would be rented. That was something.

Ali had already moved herself to this little space. She needed every bit of rent she could get from the cottage and didn't have the luxury of taking up a spot that could be earning.

She didn't see how cottage rental could pay for the Inn repairs.

## BLAIR

They sat across from one another, Joetta with a cup of coffee, Blair with sparkling water and lemon.

Blair was nauseous. She tried not to show it, but the waves of nausea hit at the most inconvenient times. Joetta pushed a plate in front of her.

"Here, just a few crackers."

Blair picked up a cracker and did as Joetta instructed.

It appeared her mother knew exactly what she needed. Of course, Blair hadn't let on that she was pregnant. She just knew.

"I saw which floor, which specialty you were headed to, so I'm just going to ask, you're not married, are you?"

Blair winced a little. "I'm not married. I actually didn't think I could get pregnant. I am uh, well, over forty years old and, well… it's a miracle in my estimation. Even though it doesn't feel too miraculous right now."

Joetta smiled. "By my calculations, that would be my fourth Kelly grandchild."

"How did you know? I mean, for a woman we thought was dead, you seem to have the numbers right."

Joetta hesitated for a moment.

Blair stared into her eyes. They were familiar, they were family. Even though they were also strangers.

"I'm good at the internet. Facebook."

"Oh, really?"

"Yeah. Thank goodness for Facebook. But I've been keeping track long before that. It was a lot harder to do when you were little, but these days I see the odd post of a holiday event, or a graduation."

Blair could see the pain in her eyes. Behind the carefully Botoxed forehead and the perfectly coiffed hairdo, Joetta was in pain. Blair wondered if Ali could see that at all.

It was easy to think of Ali when she was talking to Joetta. Ali looked just like Joetta. If they wanted to know how Ali would look in sixteen years, this was it.

"Well...this guy—Blake—is the baby daddy. We were living together. Things started out great, but then he got real bossy and real lazy."

Joetta gave a smile. "I know about bossy."

Blair wondered if that meant her current husband or Bruce.

"Talking about the Kelly side of things there?"

Joetta seemed to hesitate again. "I don't want to say anything bad about your father. He clearly did a beautiful job with you three girls."

*Aha, it* was *Bruce Kelly.* Of course, he bossed Joetta around; he bossed the girls around. It was his way or the highway, although if anyone was going to get their way, it was Blair. Looking at Joetta now, she wondered if the sternness he showed the most towards Ali wasn't because she was the oldest but because she looked so much like Joetta? The unfairness of that tore at Blair's heart.

Blair decided to be blunt; who knew how many chances she'd get to talk to this woman?

"So...can I ask you—how you did it? How did you stay away?"

"Well, I didn't have a choice. I was sixteen when I met Bruce. Your father was handsome—totally different from any boy I'd ever dated. He was a grown-up man. A Vietnam vet."

Blair wondered today what people would think about that. Her father was a man, and sixteen is a girl.

Joetta jumped in, seeming to read her thoughts.

"It wasn't like that. He had just turned twenty. I was almost seventeen. His age wasn't the problem with my parents, but the wrong side of the track? The wrong side of the beach? *That* was a problem."

There was no mistaking Bruce Kelly as a tough guy. Maybe that was romantic to a teenager. Blair could see how it had changed as Bruce aged.

"Once upon a time, I thought I loved him very much."

Blair couldn't believe she was getting this information.

"You were sixteen," Blair said. She remembered a boy she thought she loved when she was sixteen.

"Yes, with a silver spoon in my mouth up until it was Hamburger Helper," Joetta said that lightly, more a dig at herself, and not at the lifestyle that Bruce and his daughters lived.

"Obviously, then your family was well-to-do, right? I mean, we found these dresses and pretty jewelry. Dad had put them in a box in the attic at the house."

"Yes, I was. Well, my parents were. I was expected to follow a certain path. But I made a lot of mistakes that I couldn't come back from."

Blair pictured a young girl, in trouble, scared. Her mother was a scared teen. That's how she'd begun her grown-up life, before she was ready.

"I guess I should also tell you some of the why of it. I didn't thrive in Toledo, and Bruce didn't really appreciate the skills that I had, which were home décor, fashion...not helpful things if you want to get an actual job. Soon, my afternoon Tom Collins turned into…Tom Collinses."

Joetta paused and then said with a clear voice and with clear eyes, "I am an alcoholic."

Blair felt her connection with her mother was stronger than she even realized. Blair knew she, too, could never drink again if she wanted the best for her baby.

Joetta went on.

"The three of you were in the car, and I was drunk, and I crashed it. I wound up with some injuries, but miraculously, you three came out without a scratch. I imagine Ali strapped you in; certainly, I didn't. Then came the drunk tank at the jail—your father picked the three of you up. And that was the last time I saw you. Well, that was the last time I could see you, and you would know I was there."

*What did she mean by that?*

Blair choked back some tears, reached out a hand. For the first time, she imagined an entirely different story from the one she and her sisters had believed to be true. In that story, Bruce was the stoic widower. In this story, Joetta was the banished princess.

"But after you got sober, why not then?"

"Well, even then, your father didn't trust that I was a safe space for his three daughters. And I guess I wasn't."

Joetta closed her eyes, and a tear slipped down her cheek.

"I guess we have something in common."

Blair looked at her mother. Joetta's face was softer now as the two just sat together, looking at each other. Marveling in something entirely new.

Joetta spoke.

"I think you have my eyes but a Kelly jawline. Which is enviable and quite impressive."

"Well, maybe. But I was thinking about something else. I'm looking for an AA meeting here in Florida."

Joetta winced. Blair felt bad then, to blame her for the alcohol problem.

"I didn't mean to say that I think my drinking is your fault. It's all me."

"Genetic too, though. So, well, okay, there are a couple of options."

Joetta got out a pen and paper and started writing down some meeting locations. Her mother was sober, and somehow that was a huge ray of hope for Blair. She could do this, too.

Blair felt better. For the very first time in her life, Blair had a mother—at the very moment she was trying to learn how to be a mother herself.

# Eighteen

FAYE

Faye couldn't believe it, but with her three assistants and Rudy Palmer's truck, they wound up making the deadline for the wedding. And she didn't think her creations looked half bad!

They unloaded all of the centerpieces, and she tended to each one on her own. She placed them on the tables; she walked around and looked at each. She wanted them to look good 360-degrees!

And then it was time to make sure the bride had what she wanted. That would be the true test. Faye hoped that seeing the bride's Pinterest was enough of a guideline to estimate what the woman would want for her big day. But it was a huge gamble. Pinterest and real life never did exactly exist on the same planet.

Faye briefly flashed back to her own wedding. Faye was not a blushing bride back in her day. If any of them had had a traditional wedding, it was for sure Ali. Ali had a church and a hall, and a professional photographer.

Faye had irritated the heck out of Ali when she and Sawyer's dad did the whole courthouse marriage. Ali did throw her a lovely reception after the fact; Ali always did what she could to make Blair and Faye happy.

But over the years, of course, she'd been to weddings. She loved flowers, so hopefully—fingers crossed——the bouquet featuring ranunculus, peony, and sweet pea would be a hit. In the end, flower arranging was more art than science—and beauty, no question, in the eye of the beholder.

*The bride, Cheyanne Bridges, better be flexible*, Faye thought, *because this was for sure a hiccup on the way to the perfect wedding.* Flowers from a woman who'd crossed her fingers and punted. Flowers from a floral designer who was making it up as she went, and, uh, *wasn't* a floral designer!

She hoped Cheyanne liked them and that Rudy's business didn't suffer if she didn't. One of Rudy's staff had said something about influencers in the wedding party? *Good lord.*

Of course, it was the actual floral designer who had let Cheyanne Bridges down, but quibbling over who was at fault on a woman's wedding day had to be bad luck for everyone involved!

Faye decided the best thing to do was just take full responsibility. If this were a mess, the poor, sick floral designer wouldn't get blamed, and neither would Rudy. Who cares if her five-minute stint as a floral arranger came to naught? She was doing this as a favor. She'd take the hit if it sucked.

"Hello. I know we've never met," she introduced herself, "but your floral designer had an unexpected emergency."

"Why didn't someone call me and tell me?" Cheyanne said.

"Well, that I don't know, we just wanted to be sure you had a good day."

"I really wish someone would have given me the heads up." Cheyanne Bridges was about to cry!

*Uh oh.*

"Don't cry, you'll mess up that perfect makeup. Now, really focus on this bouquet. Let me know how we can make this better.

I'm right here. And we can run back to the greenhouse. You still have an hour before—"

"—Stop, okay, just let me, uh." Cheyanne waved her hands by her eyes to stop the liquid from messing up the airbrushed makeup. Faye handed her a folded tissue. Cheyanne appeared to pull it together and then did as Faye suggested; she really looked at the flowers.

She delicately fingered the sweet pea. She picked up the bouquet and put the arrangement in front of her dress. She stood at the mirror, and all the while, a photographer was snapping away. It was slightly annoying—it was like the wedding paparazzi.

Soon, a tumble of bridesmaids and a cacophony of giggles filled the little tent on the beach set up for the final "get ready" photos of the bride and her girls.

"My goodness," Faye said and put her hands on her ears.

"I know, right? They can be loud," Cheyanne said.

"They're gorgeous," one of the shrieks turned into discernable words.

*Gorgeous? Was the bridesmaid talking about the flowers?*

For the first time, Faye unclenched her shoulders, which had crept up to her earlobes since the moment she was presented with this floral fiasco.

Cheyanne spoke up. "They look wild, but they still fit the color scheme. How did you do it?"

Faye always loved a bit of a wild arrangement. She loved to use flowers in different ways. She loved to forage for flowering branches and leaves in her yard. She guessed a little of that was present in this bouquet.

"Well, I'm just glad you like it. I admit I did take a peek at your Pinterest to be sure of your style."

"Are you kidding me? I don't think Julie would be able to do anything like this."

That's when one of Faye's would-be assistants, Marissa, piped up. "Julie didn't. These are all hers."

"Oh my gosh," another bridesmaid piped up.

"I'm getting married in the fall. Are you—? I'm sure you're totally booked, but I just—this is so much better than what I anticipated. I want these too."

The bridesmaids giggled, drank champagne, and Faye took down the number of the next bride up for bid.

She wasn't a floral designer, but it seemed easier to just agree with the bridesmaids than to explain her life story.

Faye double-checked the arrangements at tables in the tent. She also had Marissa make sure all the family members were set with corsages and boutonnieres. She'd overestimated on that but was happy she had.

It appeared Rudy's reputation would be intact, and no one would be Yelp bombing anyone.

Faye watched the ceremony, double-checked the tables one last time, and stayed long enough to tweak anything for the main photo sessions with the wedding party. She felt satisfied that she'd done all she could for the bride's big day. Rudy sent Kyle back to get her while the other two Grotto assistants went back to the greenhouse to clean up.

And then, honestly, they celebrated their victory. Rudy had ordered pizza and pop for everyone. He offered beer, and Faye decided a cold one was in order after the whirlwind of the day.

Rudy was over the moon, it appeared!

"You guys, have you seen the reviews?" Marissa asked.

"Reviews?" Rudy asked.

"You're telling me that someone gave us a Yelp review in the middle of their wedding day?"

"That too, but here, they're tagging us in their photos. Check it out."

Marissa handed her phone to Faye; she looked at the Instagram feed, and it was her flowers. Picture after picture of her flowers! There were over a dozen photos of the flowers that she'd arranged for the Bridges' wedding.

*#BridgeOfLoveThatThingOfCourse*
*#ForeverWedding*
*#GottaGrottoFlowers*
*#bestfloradesigner*

"I mean—I like to grow flowers. I like to put them in vases. But 'floral designer'—that sounds a little bit fancy."

"Well, fancy or not, you could make a fortune doing that out here. Your stuff is—it's just original and different from any of the other floral designers that we've had coming in and out of our workshop," Rudy said.

Faye was floored. *What in the world?*

"Do you want to put out your shingle? I could be your supplier."

"Well, that's an interesting idea. Can you really make money as a floral designer?"

"Floral designers usually buy wholesale from us, then the brides pay half as a deposit and half after the event. The bride's father asked me who to pay, and I told him to pay me, and I would take care of it. But it's not mine. What's your Venmo?"

She shared her Venmo profile, and Faye's phone immediately buzzed a notification that money had been deposited in her account.

She looked at the number. "You have got to be kidding me. This is after paying for the stock?"

"No joke. Now stand by for the gratuity they added." Faye looked at the numbers again. *This was cash money, great money!*

"Give the gratuity to Kyle, Marrissa, and Jordan." She returned it to Rudy's Venmo.

Rudy nodded, and it was done.

All of a sudden, the idea of being a fancy floral designer took hold in Faye's imagination. What a second act—combining what she loved the most, floral design, with what she needed: money.

# Nineteen

## BLAIR

Blair looked at her phone. There were literally dozens of missed calls and six messages. She'd been ignoring them in the weeks she'd been gone.

The messages started out angry:

*Where are you? I can't believe you've done this. How am I gonna pay the rent without you? You're the one who has the savings account information. How could you do this to me?*

Then:

*Please come back. We can work this out.*

And finally:

*I'm sorry. I get the point. I need to be better. Come back.*

*You're being a witch. This is crazy. I'm so glad I'm rid of you.*

*I'm sorry. Let's talk.*

Blake had gone from messaging several times a day to once a day. Hopefully, that was a pattern that would continue until he stopped calling altogether. He continued to cycle through anger, appeasement, apology, anger. *Ugh.* She had left a mess, that was for sure.

She knew she had something to tell him. She knew he had every right to know. But that said, she wasn't ready. She wanted to have that first doctor's appointment to make sure everything was OK. And everything *was* OK. So now she was trying to concoct another reason to delay the conversation she didn't want to have.

How would Blake take the news that she was pregnant? And how would Blake take the news that she didn't want him to have anything to do with raising their baby?

It was those questions that swirled around her mind as she sat on the deck of the Blueberry Bungalow. Darla had curled up and decided to perch on her feet. Better than a little throw blanket. She lightly scratched the spot behind Darla's ears that the kitty made clear was her only approved spot to pet.

Blair turned the issue over and over. She knew she had to tell Blake, and she knew he probably would want some sort of role as a father. But she also knew getting away from him was a good idea.

There was so much unresolved here in Florida with her immediate family situation, but even so, she was getting stronger. She was healthier. She was more in control. She was making her own decisions and managing her own money, not having money come out of the debit card that she wasn't aware of until it was too late. That had gotten old. And she'd gotten out with some cash, but not enough. She would probably need child support until the hotel and cottages were up and earning.

That meant telling Blake, soon.

Her new friend showed up on her little deck.

"Well, it's a Knight in Shining Track Shoes!"

"Sir Ford of Haven Beach. And here you are," he said.

Ford looked like he'd just finished a run on the beach. She had joined him a couple of times for a very slow stroll since her inauspicious fainting spell. She'd not passed out again; this was a win!

"And there you are."

"I thought I would check in on my dehydrated, new friend."

She lifted up a glass of water with ice in it that also contained a lovely lemon and jiggled it in his general direction.

"Well, that's good. At least I can rest easy that you're paying attention to your hydration."

"I am."

"This place is kind of adorable," Ford said.

"It is. Turns out I'm one of three owners."

"Really? So, you're a hotel magnate? Pass the champagne!"

"More like a surprise heir, I guess. Somehow, our mother left this to us when she died. Except now our mother's not dead."

"That sounds epic."

"And I appreciate your solicitous attitude toward me, but along with being pregnant, I am a brand-new, freshly minted alcoholic in recovery."

She'd taken a page out of Joetta's book. Her mother had taught her something about her disease. Own it. Don't hide it. She felt incredibly lighter after being direct.

"That's exactly the kind of new friend I was looking for, brutally honest, a cheap date, and one who very soon won't be able to beat me in a foot race."

"Don't count on that race thing. I ran track in high school. I might decide to school you."

"I welcome the education, and congratulations. That's pretty exciting. Amazing, actually."

She smiled. He was genuinely happy for her—this new friend. And he was right. It was exciting. Even though everything around her was topsy-turvy, increasingly the idea of becoming a mother to this little nugget was filling her with joy.

# Twenty

## ALI

Ali was determined to handle the problem. She didn't know how, but she also knew she had lured her sisters to this place. Faye had impulsively taken a retirement package, and Blair had run from her life in Cincinnati. Plus, Blair had a baby on the way! She knew that in part, they were convinced that The Sea Turtle was the end of the rainbow.

But it wasn't. There were major storm clouds brewing, and Ali had to stop them. For the first time in her life, she felt like she had made the wrong choice when it came to protecting her family.

She'd led them astray instead of helping them stay on course.

She wasn't sure what she was going to tell them. How much of this could they handle? Ali decided to tell them a partial truth, for now. She would slow-play the facts in hopes that she could figure out a solution.

It was sunset—time for the Grand Finale.

She thought that would be as good a time as any. After the

guests had watched the mango sun slowly slip behind the horizon, the cottage guests made their way back to the Key Lime.

This left Blair, Faye, and Ali on the three Adirondack chairs that Sawyer kept out for them. *We ought to enjoy the beach as much as we can, as long as we have it*, Ali thought but didn't say.

Blair was nursing water with lemon. Faye and Ali enjoyed a sangria that Ali had made for today's Grand Finale. The guests had loved it.

Faye spoke first. "OK, sis. Clearly something's happening. What's up?"

"Well, you know we had the inspection—"

Blair piped up. "Oh, right, the one that will let us know what needs to be done for the Inn."

"Yeah, that's the one."

"How bad off are we?" Faye asked.

"Well, here's the thing, the cottages, are inhabitable, so that's good. But we really can't live in the Inn right now while I handle the repairs." Ali didn't know if she could handle the repairs. She also hated the fact that she'd dragged them here, and now, she was going to kick them out in a manner of speaking.

Blair spoke up. "Well, how are you gonna pay for the repairs if you're not getting much rent from the cottages, because we're free-loading in them?"

The sisters weren't freeloading, but they *were* all three living there rent-free.

"Well, that I'm not sure. But I can't have you in the Inn while it's not safe."

"I'll find my own place," Faye jumped in immediately. "Actually, there's an apartment above the Grotto that Rudy showed me the other day."

Ali raised an eyebrow at Faye. "Oh, he did?"

Blair giggled at Ali's gentle teasing of their middle sister's potential romantic entanglement.

"It's not that way. You guys, I am going to be a floral designer!"

Faye told them about her impromptu career shift and success. Ali was beaming with pride. Of course, Faye was good at floral design. She'd always had an incredible eye for it.

"Anyway, living about the stock I need seems prudent. I'm sure that's a perfect solution. Rent out my cottage, that means four to rent."

"Five, I'm going to be bunking in the office." Ali had already decided that much. She'd sleep on a cot she'd discovered in the storage room and shower in the pool house.

"I can move too...I just don't have access to too much cash right now," Blair looked very worried, and it broke Ali's heart.

*Nope. No way was this going to fall on her.*

"We got you," Faye squeezed Blair's hand.

"Guys, I am not picky. I could bunk with you, Ali."

The two older sisters looked at each other and smiled. Their baby sister wasn't picky—but she was used to being taken care of. Ali liked taking care of her sisters and felt like she was failing.

She didn't know how long they'd last here anymore, but she decided the rental from one cottage wouldn't make or break them.

"You're staying in the Blueberry. You're looking healthy and happy, and I want my niece or nephew to cook in comfort."

"Can we afford that?" Blair asked.

"We can," Ali lied.

"So, what are the final numbers?" Faye wanted details.

Ali was afraid to give her the details, because she was also afraid that, in the end, this plan might fail. She had no idea where the money was gonna come from.

"Oh, let's not talk about this anymore. I'm still getting estimates back, and we've got our immediate issues figured out. Except for where you're gonna live. An apartment over at the nursery sounds, uh, sketchy."

"Says the woman sleeping in the office! Don't worry," Faye said. "I'll head back to the Residence Inn if I need to. Truly." Faye was confident, optimistic, and something about her seemed to glow from the inside.

*Was it Rudy Palm Tree? Or was it that she did have a nice base tan?*

Ali decided to change the subject, to get them off this topic that soon would be unavoidable.

"Floral design, even back in Toledo, you could charge good money for that. Weddings and events we did at the Frogtown Convention Center had big-ticket floral budgets."

"Right? I literally am an overnight floral design sensation." Faye told them more about how she'd saved the day for Rudy's floral designer. "Apparently, the way I arranged flowers is all the rage here in Haven Beach. My stuff was all over Instagram; turns out the wedding party was chock full of social media influencers."

Blair got out her phone and started scrolling.

"You did this? And this?"

"Yep."

"Holy moly, okay, I've got so many ideas."

"What?"

"You need an Instagram, too."

"I need an Instagram?"

"You need an Instagram. All these floral designers have fantastic Instagrams. And look at your work, it's worthy of The Gram!"

Blair continued on to explain all the marketing that they seemed to need to put into place. Blair was also supposed to do the same for The Sea Turtle. But luckily for Ali, her sisters forgot about that while they talked about Faye's new venture.

Her sisters were lost in talk about bouquets and boutonnieres, and floral arrangements of every kind.

Ali sat back. She let the conversation steer away from the problems at the Inn, and for that, she was relieved. Right now, her sisters had other things to deal with. She would deal with the problems at the Inn.

The immediate issue was solved. She had a place for Blair, and her independent middle sister, Faye, would land on her feet. Or in Rudy's rental.

After her sisters called it a night, Ali went back to the office and looked at the estimates. She'd lied about that, too. She had all the numbers she needed.

She added it up again and again.

One million. Well, eight hundred ninety thousand, to be exact. It may as well have been ten million.

If she couldn't come up with nearly a million dollars for these repairs fast, The Sea Turtle was doomed.

Her own finances were now stretched to the brink. Ted was slow rolling, giving her half the money from their house sale in Toledo, and her inheritance from dad, well, that was how she was keeping the lights on here.

Ali had her head in her hands with zero ideas and a huge headache brewing when Henry showed up in her tiny office.

She jumped a foot. She hadn't heard him come in.

"Hey, lady, this is beach life! Florida? It's supposed to be a little bit laid-back. What are you doing, burning the midnight oil?"

"Oh well, just...you know. I don't mind it. I kind of like it."

He smiled. "A lot of women around these beaches are gold-diggers—looking for the sugar daddy. That's not you."

"No, no. I have no interest in a sugar daddy. But I wouldn't mind a good rate on a loan for capital improvements."

Ali decided that if she kept talking, she'd tell Henry everything. And she wasn't ready. She feared no one would like the plan that was developing in her head.

Selling it all...

If she decided to sell, she'd have to do it with a bunch of people telling her not to. She knew Henry would tell her not to. She knew her sisters probably would too. Ted, he'd have loved the idea, but that was one good thing. He wouldn't get a dime. It was cold comfort.

Ali didn't want help or input right now; she wanted to work through it on her own. She lied. "I really appreciate that, but I can handle it."

"I've no doubt. You're one of the hardest-driving supermodels I've ever met."

"Well, and shortest, don't forget that."

Henry was too generous with the compliments. The only time Ted ever complimented her was when she decorated his university office to look like that of a real Oxford professor instead of the tiny box on the campus of the University of Toledo that it really was.

"Let's go get some dinner."

She looked at Henry. She wanted to go get dinner. She wanted to tell him everything. She wanted to reach out to her sisters. But she decided the only way she could do what she needed to do was to be cold and calculating. Money didn't lie. Numbers had no feelings.

Out to dinner with Henry wasn't gonna get the job done that she needed done. She had to do it, and she couldn't afford a distraction—much less the foundation work plainly listed on the inspection.

"You know, not tonight. I have a little bit more work to do."

"OK. You've only totally crushed my feelings. I'll recover."

Henry put his hand to his heart as though she shot him right through it.

He would be another thing she'd have to give up if they left Florida.

*Twenty-One*

## BLAIR

"Thank you, yes, got it, and I'll see you next month, yes."

When Blair had left her life in Cincinnati, she'd only hoped her boss would be patient.

Luckily, Janet Walters was a good woman and a great boss. Not only had she approved her remote work plan, but she'd also helped counsel her that it was a good idea to switch her direct deposit.

She'd stupidly allowed her income to be deposited into a joint account with Blake. He'd immediately drained it, but now, there was no more money, no more of *her* money going to that account.

Janet agreed that she could do the marketing plans and data analysis for their clients remotely. She would come back to Cinci monthly for in-person planning sessions.

This could work; she had only two paychecks and no savings, but she'd cut Blake out, and she still had her job. She actually loved marketing. Which, of course, sounded ridiculous to most people. But to Blair, it was creative. She saw it as a challenge, figuring out how to match people with the services and products from their clients. How to find the people, how to know what they needed, how to get them to act? It was a constantly changing equation that she loved solving.

She was currently looking at the metrics for Faye's new Instagram. That wasn't a paid gig, but boy, was it fun. And anything she learned about the Gulf Coast market she'd apply to The Sea Turtle.

How awesome was this remote setup that she could even take her computer out to the porch and watch the ocean in between reading demographic metric charts?

Plus, she still had health insurance. Not too glamourous, but it was key to Operation Good Mom!

Blair felt good. Sure, Faye had come to her rescue when she was in trouble, yes, she'd crashed her car, and left her life in a shambled mess, but she was clawing out. Joetta had pointed her in the right direction for AA, and she'd even been to two meetings.

You could make a mistake, and it didn't have to be the end. It didn't have to define the rest of your life.

That's when her biggest mistake crashed through her fragile self-esteem.

Blair was sitting with her computer and coffee when he showed up.

"What the hell are you doing?"

She spilled her hot coffee on her leg. It burned. She shot up out of the deck chair. But she didn't have time to deal with that pain.

"Blake?"

"You're down here, soaking up the sun, having a vacation while my life is falling apart. How selfish can one person be?"

"I'm not having a vacation." She shouldn't have to defend herself, but that's easy to say when someone attacks.

"Our account is overdrawn. You're sitting on the beach on a multi-million-dollar gold mine. And you're trying to cut me out? That's a stupid move. Very." Blake stepped closer to her and yelled right in her face. "I'm going to make your life a living hell if you keep stealing from me."

"Stealing? This isn't yours, and it isn't what you think. And my money from my work is my money. Get your own job."

Not once in their relationship had Blair said no, or stood up for herself, or punctured Blake's illusions of how great he was. Her face felt hot. The emotional scene was spiking her heart rate. She knew this was bad for the baby. But she'd had it. He had no right to talk to her this way, to demand any of her money, or stake any claims to The Sea Turtle.

"Job? I am running a company. I am the boss. And you're dropping the ball on the marketing."

"Company? Your idea is terrible. No one wants to work with you. Zero clients." Over the last few years, she'd been supportive, encouraging, in the face of one stupid business idea after another, but now she laid out the facts.

Blake stepped closer still, and it forced Blair to walk backwards.

"You don't know anything about it. You're a data geek with zero vision."

"You're pathetic, and I am tired of bankrolling your life. I took my name off the apartment lease. The rent is due, by the way."

Blake had reduced her to slinging insults just like he'd done.

He'd never hit her, but then again, she'd never called him pathetic. Too late, she realized he was cornered, neutered, and powerless, so he tried to assert power in another way.

She had good peripheral vision and saw his hand come up just in time to step back again. Unfortunately, she ran out of deck and went flying backwards.

She landed in Ford's arms.

"Stay out of this, bro." Blake snarled the words to Ford as he realized they weren't alone. And that Ford had witnessed Blake's swing and miss.

Ford helped Blair find her balance and then gently but swiftly put her behind him. He stood in front of her.

"You try to touch her again, yell anywhere in her vicinity, and you'll be missing a few teeth before you get thrown in the back of a police car."

Ford was calm, but somehow scary in his own way. Blair had zero doubt that one man was posturing, and one could back up the threat.

"I don't know who you are, but this isn't your concern."

Blair put a hand on Ford and walked forward. "Blake, get off the property. If you come back, you'll be arrested. I'll also be getting a personal protection order. So, leave, or rent will be the least of your problems."

Both men were looking at her like she'd just spoken in tongues. Blair had never heard this voice come out of her own mouth.

Somehow, she wasn't just speaking for herself, she was protecting her baby.

Any thought she had about telling Blake she was pregnant was gone. He could never know. She didn't want him near her or her baby. Ever.

Blake appeared to think about her words, at least. He seemed less likely to try to strike out again. It could have been Ford's threat or hers, but either way, Blake was outnumbered.

He could at least count to two.

"Two can play at that game. You'll be hearing from my attorney."

"You mean Bernie? He's been disbarred. Good luck with that."

Blake then hurled a choice word at her. She didn't blink.

She squelched the urge to put a hand over her tiny little bump. The last thing she wanted to do was give him a clue that they were tied together.

Forever.

# Twenty-Two

## FAYE

Blair had called her right away. But it was a different Blair. Several weeks ago, she was at rock bottom, needing her big sister to come to her rescue. This time, it was a confident Blair telling Faye she needed a lawyer and a PPO.

"This is scary." Faye knew what it was like to have a loose cannon ex.

She also had the right lawyer for the job. Faye connected Blair to Michalak, Perne, and Janco. They'd been handling legal affairs for Faye and Ali since their lives had gotten more legally complicated with divorce, retirements, inheritance, and commercial property management.

"The lawyer you recommended has let me know how to proceed. I have a witness, a neighbor saw his behavior. That's key."

"Okay, well, maybe we should move you from the cottage to a hotel. It would make me feel better."

"I'm happy at the cottage, and he's not going to ruin it. He's all bluster, and a legal document will scare him. Trust me."

It had only taken a few days to iron out the situation.

The two sisters decided not to bring Ali into it at all. They knew their sister was in *martyr mode*, as they sometimes called it.

If they told her about Blake's behavior, that would only activate Ali's mama bear instincts further. And Blair wanted to handle it. In fact, Faye was incredibly proud of how Blair was handling it. This was a new Blair. The baby of the family was developing her own mama bear side.

"But the elephant in the room, what about that?"

"I'm not telling him about the baby, nope, not doing it. And I'll figure that out later. Right now, stay healthy, stay in Florida, and bake this little muffin."

Blair had a good head on her shoulders, and somehow being pregnant had pushed her from being the baby of the family into being a formidable and decisive woman. It was so impressive to see her take charge of her life.

Also, Faye was excited. It had been so long since they'd had a baby in the family. Woe to the man who caused her future niece or nephew one ounce of stress!

To celebrate her newfound voice, Blair had invited Faye to lunch at the coffee shop in Anna Mara. This was a few towns over from Haven Beach, but wow, it was about as cute a beach town as Haven Beach.

Faye had a lot of work to do for the floral business, but it paid to see a lot of the little venues and towns on the Gulf Side.

And if Blair in charge was a novelty, it could wear off. Faye would ride the wave while it lasted.

As Faye walked into the tiny little cafe, she thought, *Well, this is about as fancy as it gets.* The room had the whiff of old-money, old-style Florida flair.

Faye thought this would be just the type of place that their dad would hate. But Blair loved a posh lunch. Faye just hoped she was dressed well enough for the occasion. Blair had mentioned that maybe this cafe could be a good future client for Faye's budding floral arranging business.

As Faye walked into the pale sherbet-colored room, she saw her baby sister at the table. Blair waved. Faye nodded and headed over. The two sisters greeted each other, and Faye had an immediate sense that Blair was up to something.

"This is about the fanciest lunch we've had in some time."

"I know, right? Bruce would hate this place."

"Yeah, he would."

Their dad did not spend time having coffee or tea. If he were going to do leisure, it would be on a boat with a fishing rod, not on a green with a golf club, or in a restaurant with a tasting menu.

"So, I don't know how you're gonna react, but I think...I think you'll be OK. I think what I'm about to tell you is important," Blair said.

*We've just gotten through the bombshell of the pregnancy and Blake. What now?*

"What could possibly be today's bombshell?" Faye asked. "We've had enough lately, don't you think?"

"Well, today's bombshell is right behind you."

Faye turned around to find their mother—smiling, but clearly nervous and hoping to sit in the third chair set up at the table.

"Oh, man. That's why we're here?"

This was in direct opposition to what Ali wanted, what she'd ordered them to do. Ali wanted no part of Joetta, and she had every right to feel that way. Faye had never once gone behind Ali's back, and she felt that this might be the ultimate betrayal, sitting with Joetta.

Faye rubbed her temples. She felt a headache was imminent.

"Hi. I know I have no right to have lunch with you," Joetta said. She stood there at their table, looking tiny and vulnerable.

Faye didn't want to make a scene. She didn't want a family drama to play out in the middle of this swanky public space.

"Lunch, fine, sit, please." Faye gestured for Joetta to sit in the empty chair. Joetta gracefully took a seat.

Looking at Joetta, she reminded Faye so much of Ali. It was hard not to have an open heart. She was clearly their blood.

*Lunch—we can do lunch,* thought Faye. She tried to relax her shoulders but knew she was coiled, ready for something to crash. She focused on Joetta, this woman from their past. She'd been a fable, a sweet perfume in the mist of her memory, a blurry picture that Faye couldn't grab hold of no matter how many times she tried. And yet here she was. The perfume was the same.

Faye noticed how delicate their mother was. Refined. So different from what Bruce Kelly brought to their DNA mix.

"I'm not telling Ali this. I don't think Ali's ready for any of it," Blair said.

"No, she's not. She made it pretty clear that she doesn't want to have anything to do with Joetta. And doesn't want us to either," Faye added.

Joetta nodded. "She has every right to feel that. I have no rights whatsoever."

That made Faye feel guilty somehow. *No rights.*

"I think you should hear our mother's side of the story," Blair said.

It was hard to think that their mother could have a side of the story that was worth listening to. She'd left them high and dry. Well—maybe not high and dry. All his gruffness aside, Bruce did provide for them. He was a stable influence. He loved them, even though he didn't express it until he was dying. That was a lesson. Remembering that put Faye in a better mindset. No one lives forever. Any moment it could be too late.

Faye spoke. "It was Mommy. We didn't call her mother." Faye's voice wavered.

She realized that Blair had no negative associations—or positive associations, for that matter—with the woman at the table.

Blair had grown up with Ali as a mother, and Faye as a stand-in for Ali when needed. Of the three of them, Blair was truly motherless.

Until now. Blair needed a mother; even though they'd done their best, they, too, were children.

Faye realized that Blair was the most susceptible to letting Joetta into her life, especially now, as she tapped into her own maternal instincts.

"So, what happened? I don't want to be mean, but I'm a mother, I cannot ever imagine leaving my son, ever." Faye felt a fierce loyalty to Ali at that moment, and to Ali's betrayed sense of what had happened.

"I didn't want to leave. It wasn't my idea."

Faye looked at Blair, who reached a hand out to Joetta and nodded for her to continue.

"I don't want to be talking bad about Bruce. I mean, he was a big lug, but he was our dad. He did the best he could," Faye said.

*But had he?* Faye was questioning so much now.

"Oh, I know that," Blair replied, "He was a good dad. I just… there's just…well, can you just listen?"

Blair was doing a full-court press for Joetta. And Faye, who did not have as strong a position as Ali did, thought there was an open door—or at least a cracked window—for some sort of relationship. It seemed impossible right now. Faye was in the middle and always tried to see both sides. This, though? This one was a doozy.

"OK, I'll listen. But this better not get back to Ali. Ever. Do you understand?"

"Of the three of you…she knows the most. I had a drinking problem. Faye, you saw a little of it, I suppose, but Ali, was the adult back then, not me."

Faye had flashes of Mommy sleeping. Mommy with "the flu." Mommy falling down.

But they were only flashes. Ali, two years older, probably did know so much more.

Joetta then produced a folded-up piece of stationery, tucked neatly in a matching envelope.

She slid a letter to Faye. Faye scanned it. It was from Joetta to Bruce.

"I was trying to convince him to let me bring you here. I had the means then. I was sober."

It was dated 1984, several weeks *after* Faye thought her mother had passed.

She read the words. It was heartbreaking. The letter was full of promises and pleading. Faye could feel the pain that Joetta had been going through.

At the end of the letter, there was Bruce Kelly's unmistakable handwriting. Faye shook her head. Faye looked at the envelope: it was a return to sender from Florida to Toledo and back here again. This showed how hard Joetta tried to stay in their lives.

But it was more than that. The letter showed how well Bruce had succeeded at keeping her out. She read her father's note:

*If you continue to harass us, I will expose your secrets to everyone in your new life in Florida. I know you had a fancy wedding. And I know you're living off your rich husband and snooty mom and dad. I have read all about it in the society pages. Good. Stay away—or I will make sure they know what happened. The gossip pages would eat up the stories I have.*

Faye swallowed hard. Bruce was not kidding. He was mean as a snake when he needed to be. She went back in her memories to Mommy and Daddy, in the kitchen, in the backyard, in the car. Daddy was scary, strict, quiet. Faye could easily see how Joetta would be terrified reading this letter.

"You wanted to come back?"

"I wanted to come back from the second I left. More than that —I didn't want to leave. I mean, Bruce and I had our problems, and I definitely had my problems, but I wanted to work them out. I love you three. I love you."

Tears were rolling down the perfectly made-up complexion of

Joetta Armstrong. Faye saw her struggle to keep that perfect posture. For the first time, Faye could see the years on this woman, the strain of all of this.

Faye didn't know where it came from, because it was so unlike her, but she felt tears well up in her own eyes. Something rolled through her body. She thought she would have to run and get out of this restaurant. It would be horrifying to break down in public.

Joetta, smoothly—without even being seen—was by her side. She had somehow shifted to sit right next to her now. She put an arm around her, tentatively at first. And then she squeezed Faye's shoulders.

She smelled sweet; Mommy always smelled so pretty.

And that was all she needed, that pretty memory of Mommy. That little hug.

This was her mother. Mommy was here. She was alive. Mommy never wanted to leave!

Faye wasn't a middle-aged woman in that moment; she was an abandoned child getting the second chance she'd prayed for every night of her life.

# Twenty-Three

## ALI

Ali had taken three more bids for repairs. One was higher, one was lower, but a search of the latter company afterwards revealed they had over a dozen complaints against them from the Better Business Bureau. The third quote was competitive but couldn't begin work for over a year.

Keeping the Inn empty for a year? They'd all be bankrupt if that were the timeline! Meanwhile, she was pretty sure her clothes were starting to smell moldy from living in the storage closet of the office.

There was one ray of light, and that was the cottages. Ali continued doing the repairs and upgrades. Her new best friend was YouTube. Every time she was tempted to "call a guy," she watched a how-to video instead.

In one week, they were fully booked at the cottages and would be for the entire summer. That was powering her through her work, solo, at The Sea Turtle.

That was the good side of the equation.

Blair was even pushing for Instagram and TikTok accounts to market the cottages into next year.

"We could even document the progress of bringing the Inn back to life. I mean, what a hook? Sinatra slept here, and we're restoring it to the Rat Pack Glory!"

Blair was enthusiastic, but Ali kept thinking, *What if we find actual rats?* And there still wasn't money to pull the trigger on the reno.

Ali didn't want to quit, so she forged ahead, hoping the math would change.

In the midst of all that, she'd had a tense call with Ted.

"Tye wants to go abroad, and I am in support of it. He'll need that experience if he wants to be a well-rounded candidate for grad school."

"In theory, that's great, but how much are we talking here?"

"It's not something to put a price on Ali. You're so pedestrian on this."

"Pedestrian? We're not rich, Ted."

"Oh, really? I was there, Ali. I know. You're sitting on a ton of real estate, and now you're being miserly about our son's future. I'd say that's a bad look, Ali, a very bad look."

She channeled Faye in that moment and gave it to him with both barrels.

"You know what's a bad look, Ted? Your gold chain and untucked dress shirt when you cruise around in that mid-life crisis mobile, *that's* the bad look. I'll talk to Tye myself. And if it's so important, you pay for our son's Grand Tour. A month ago, he wanted to be a sportscaster, and this month, he's an architect. I don't see how spending tens of thousands of dollars is the solution. He should be learning a trade!" Ted was against welder, plumber, and electrician—

all jobs Ali was convinced Tye would be great at and better than his current plan to tour Europe.

With that, she hung up. She'd talk to her children without Ted as a middleman.

That was how she did things with her daughter Katie. They were so much closer now. She knew Katie's dreams and goals and was determined to help her future designer daughter in any way she could—but, again, not with blank checks. That was off the table. Both of her kids needed less of Ted's resume-building life advice, in her opinion.

She was about to call Tye when her phone started pinging.

It was the reservation system app she used to book guests. *Ooh, maybe we're getting more bookings?!*

She opened the app, and there was cancellation after cancellation.

"What in the world?"

The five guests they had coming next week canceled, and then five more for the next month.

What was happening? Maybe the app was malfunctioning? She had no idea. Blair was her marketing and tech guru.

Ali didn't want to lay problems on her pregnant sister's doorstep, but something was wrong, and they needed to fix it.

Fast.

Twenty-Four

## BLAIR

Blair finished analyzing the data of a brand awareness campaign for her day job. She summarized the key points, sent them to Janet, and then closed her laptop.

She thought about her big sister.

She knew Ali was in *do-it-all-alone* mode, but that couldn't go on. She and Faye had seen how Ali looked—tired, stressed, and not dissimilar to the way she'd appeared when they were still in Toledo.

This was supposed to be an amazing family business. Right now, it was all on her big sister's shoulders.

Admittedly, Blair realized that her entire life, she had never taken the brunt of any responsibility in her family. She let Ali and then Faye take care of her. And to some degree, she had expected a series of bad-choice boyfriends to do the same. It was almost hilarious that she'd expected Blake to take care of her. Looking back, Blake and her were two people totally stunted in a twenty-something mentality when they met.

But not anymore; at least in her case.

She felt galvanized by the mission she now had. She was going to take care of this little life. She'd always thought of her sisters as the Lionesses or the Mama Bears, and herself as a cub. That was over, and long overdue, actually. She shuddered to think about what her sisters really thought of her. If she looked back, she realized they'd done so much, too much. The baby of the Kelly Girls was babied too long. And now, well, she'd have a baby of her own.

Blair decided it was time to show Ali she could be counted on, too. Blair went out to find her big sister and insist she be given some sort of task today to help The Sea Turtle. She wasn't going to get on ladders or lift wheelbarrows full of sand, but there had to be something she could do.

Before she found Ali, she took a quick walk along the paths of The Sea Turtle resort complex. Ali saw regs and codes to manage, Faye saw landscaping and plants, but Blair saw stories she could tell when she was marketing this place. Hundreds of vacation stories to help bring in bookings. She resisted the urge to rub her palms together in anticipation, like Mr. Burns on *The Simpsons*!

The place was so amazing—each cottage with its own distinct colors. And thanks to Katie, they had a plan on how to decorate each of the cottages. Ali had been so busy with the boring infrastructure stuff, that the fun decorating touches had been neglected for the last four cottages. So, Katie had done a mood board for each cottage, and the Kelly sisters would thrift or craft all of the different décor elements of each space. That was it—maybe she could go thrifting?

The idea immediately brought Mommy to mind. Before, when they thought their mother was dead, Ali would give credit for their thrifting gene to their mother. Right now, they didn't mention Joetta Armstrong in Ali's presence. Ali was totally closed off.

Blair would work on it, an inch at a time. Someday...

With thrifting in her brain, Blair headed to the office.

If Ali didn't have a chore for her, she was going to take the mood board for the Blueberry Bungalow and work on sourcing items to realize Katie's vision.

As usual, Ali was at work—this time in the office. She was on the phone, and things didn't sound like they were going very well.

"But this is unprecedented. How can they have—no, I thought we had some sort of protection for cancellations. Trial period? No? Hello?"

Ali put her head in her hands. Her big sister was looking stressed. She had more lines on her face than Joetta these days.

"Hey," Blair said softly, "what's today's crisis?"

"I am trying to deal with this without stressing you out, but..."

"I just heard you have some sort of tense conversation with someone. You can't protect me from everything. I'm a big girl."

"But you're pregnant, and you've got enough to deal with. You do not need to be dealing with the stress of running this place."

"Sis, what's going on?"

Ali sighed again. "All right. Well, you know we were booked for the next four weeks straight?"

"Yes."

"We're not anymore. We have no bookings. I had—let's see, four times five—that's over twenty cancellations that came in during the last ninety minutes or so."

Blair couldn't believe that.

"Yeah," Ali continued. "I've got this app for our rentals, and I pay a lot of money for it. I thought maybe it had gone down, but they're saying no. All these people have canceled."

"Do they lose deposits?"

"They all did it in plenty of time. And also, I guess I'm on some sort of probationary period, so I don't have all the services the app provides."

"That's crap."

"Yeah, agreed. I just don't know what to do next."

"Why did they all cancel?"

Ali shrugged and Blair saw her jaw tighten. Her big sister was trying not to cry. It killed Blair to see Ali so upset, and to believe she was in it alone.

"I'm on it," Blair said, straightening up. "Give me the logins. Marketing—that's my area. If you won't let me paint different houses or roll out the cabanas with Sawyer, you've got to give me the computer."

Ali cocked her head. She looked Blair up and down, trying to see the adult maybe, instead of the child? Who knows, but Blair was tired of being typecast as the useless one. She was going to pull her weight around here. She leveled a gaze at Ali and didn't blink.

"OK, fine. Here's the login information. I have no idea what's going on, but I don't see any way around what just happened. At this point, we have zero income coming in, and you know how important that is for all the things we need to do."

"I do know. You concern yourself with something else on the list of the many things you need to do—and I'll take care of the booking app. I'll investigate how in the world we went from booked to no bookings in the blink of an eye."

"OK, but then promise me you'll only do this for a couple of hours. I don't want you to be overly stressed."

"I'm not overly stressed. Don't worry. I promise I'm taking care of myself."

"All right—and that little nugget?"

"Yes, and this little nugget." The thought of the future nugget did put a smile on Ali's face. That was something.

She left Ali to stress out over something else and went back to her cottage, logins in hand. She started doing a few searches.

It looked like all the people that had been canceling on the app had complied with the rules. They'd all canceled in the right amount of time—but something had to have sparked it.

She searched for *The Sea Turtle* on Google Reviews, and there it was—the world's most detailed list of all the issues that had happened when Ted was here. Food disasters, plumbing, insects; it sounded like The Sea Turtle was in the midst of an Old Testament plague! But all of the reviews had just appeared in the last day.

And they'd later found out those issues were caused by Ted himself.

*Could that be it? Had Ted torpedoed The Sea Turtle, again?*

Maybe. Blair didn't want to do it, but she went to Yelp, and sure enough, those bad reviews had been copied and pasted. There were some variations, but it appeared as though someone had run the bad reviews through ChatGPT and spit out some paraphrasing of the same vile accusations against The Sea Turtle.

"OK, now we know—we've been bombed."

It was one thing to know what had happened. It was another to fix it. And to prevent it from happening again.

Blair decided the next step was to get rid of those reviews so they could salvage something of the season.

Luckily, Blair knew how to manage a marketing disaster.

# *Twenty-Five*

## FAYE

Somehow Faye's second career, the one that had fallen into her lap, was going amazingly well. She'd done the surprise wedding, and thanks to Blair's marketing and social media word of mouth, she was booking up.

She looked at her calendar. She had booked four weddings! And Erica Bell had hired her to provide a weekly flower arrangement for The Morning Bell.

She had moved into the Residence Inn, temporarily but immediately. She'd decided moving into the Grotto was maybe sending more of a "girlfriend" message than she was able to back up.

She had a house to empty out and sell in Toledo, and this was a temporary solution, but she had two rooms, one for Sawyer when and if he needed one. It wasn't economical or permanent, but it would be fine for now. Her buyout would sustain her a while and the house sale would be the next well she dropped a bucket in.

Faye's bottom line would be healthy and then the big floral

money would come rolling in. She chuckled at the idea that flowers was a job. *Yay!*

Rudy was set to pick her up to take her to some flower wholesalers. Faye headed down to the lobby to keep an eye out for Rudy's truck.

The Florida heat was just fine by her. After a lifetime of wind that chilled her bones, a little sultry weather was in order. Since they were looking at flowers, she'd selected her best low, straight, slightly baggy jeans, and a Tony Packo's t-shirt. If they were looking at flowers, they'd likely buy flowers and that meant pots with dirt. This life did not require formalwear and that suited her perfectly too!

She was so different from their mother. Joetta was formal, she was designer handbags, she was refined. They'd met for the lunch that first time, and then again, one on one. It wasn't easy or breezy, but it was a start. They were getting to know each other. Joetta had asked after Sawyer.

*Sawyer.* Faye wondered how he'd take the news.

Sawyer was an artist, that was becoming clear. *Was that somewhere in Joetta's family? Is that where he got it?*

So many things were going well. Her floral design startup, her burgeoning relationship with Joetta, and even the way Blair was handling her challenges. Faye had picked up a broken Blair back in Ohio. But today, glowing was the word for her baby sister.

But it wasn't all sunshine and roses. Ali would see their relationship with Joetta as a betrayal. As sure as the blacktop could melt your flipflops around here, her sister would be crushed to learn they'd started up with Joetta.

Ali was her biggest worry. Things had flipped upside down. She'd been worried about Blair and now, well, it seemed like Ali was headed for disaster. If the Joetta situation didn't do it, the stress of the repairs to the Inn could very well pull her under.

Ali was keeping something from them. Faye was sure of it. Yes, they were lying about meeting with Joetta, but Ali was lying too.

Faye continued to reach out to Ali, but Ali kept saying she had everything handled. That was Ali.

The worry had shown up on Faye's face, and she totally didn't notice Rudy until he lightly tapped the horn of his truck.

"Whoa, quite the serious face. Get in and tell me all about it."

This was another thing that oddly and unexpectedly was going right. Rudy Palm Tree.

They'd been spending a lot of time together. He'd helped her set prices for her work, helped her understand the overhead she'd have, shared his thoughts on what was local and in season here, and shared his Rolodex of resources too.

This was easy and breezy. And every once in a while, there was a spark of something else.

"Well, let's see, I'm worried about my sister."

"Blair? She has that PPO. And if there's even a whiff of that loser ex, you have me on speed dial."

"Ha, thank you, but no, it's Ali. She's just really trying to do the Inn all by herself. And it's getting to be a problem. No one can do it all alone, you know?"

"I know. I actually don't know what I would have done without you. Lately."

"What?"

"I mean, we'd have been trashed by the social media crowd if you'd not done that wedding. And then, well, you helped me manage my staff shortage issues with your ninja shop steward skills, and also, if it's not too forward to say, looking at you in the jeans and t-shirt there, well, I'm not gonna lie. You make me feel young."

"Young?"

"Yeah, like forty, maybe forty-five."

Faye laughed so hard she snorted and then was slightly embarrassed by the snort and laughed some more.

And then she stopped laughing and darn it if she wasn't staring into Rudy's eyes. This time neither of them was laughing.

Things had turned romantic, right there in the front of the Grotto pickup truck.

Neither of them said another word, and they met in the middle for a big, juicy, not so old, kiss.

Faye was slightly dizzy after they separated.

"Well, well, well, Rudy Palm Tree. You kiss like a much younger man as well."

"Yeah, how young?"

"Hmm, thirty-nine, maybe thirty-nine-and-a-half?"

This time he laughed loud and from his chest.

They heard a very loud honking noise and realized they'd been blocking the lobby entrance with their mini make-out session.

"Yeah, yeah, I'm on it," Rudy said and waved his hand out the window.

He put the truck in gear, and they rolled out toward the wholesalers.

As he drove, Faye reached her hand out and placed it in the middle of the seat. Rudy's hand met hers, and they held hands like kids as they drove.

She may not be young, but today at least, Rudy had helped her feel alive, optimistic, and like moving to Haven Beach was one of the best ideas Ali had ever come up with.

Now if only Ali could remember the same!

*Twenty-Six*

## ALI

Ali realized she was beyond stressed out. She realized she needed help. She realized the whole point of being in Florida was to enjoy Florida.

With Blair on the case of the mysterious mass cancellation, Ali also realized she hadn't eaten much over the last few days. She also hadn't seen Henry very often, so for once, she decided to step away from The Sea Turtle and spend some time with him. She'd begged off multiple times when he'd offered to hang out. Lately she realized nothing in her life was bringing her any joy. Just a few short weeks ago, everything at The Sea Turtle brought her joy.

Was it a sign that she needed to pull the plug? She was close. Maybe it was just the perfect time to walk over to the Seashell Shack to reconnect with the reasons she was here and reconnect with the man who'd been nothing but kind and welcoming. And walk she did.

To her shame, Ali realized it had been days and days since she'd stopped and really inhaled the salt air. It had been just as long since she'd had her toes in the sand.

Ali walked along the beach and immediately the woes of the last few weeks felt less woeful.

It was midday, the hot sun was probably putting sun wrinkles on top of worry wrinkles, but she didn't care. She needed some vitamin D. Her feet sank into the hot sand, so she inched closer to the water as it rolled onto the shore in soft waves. It was a beautiful day.

Luckily, Hank's restaurant was only a block away. Though she could have strolled for hours, there were tasks to accomplish. A quick lunch ray or two would have to do.

She got to the back area of the Seashell Shack, and sure enough, it was hopping with tourists and locals enjoying the lunch menu.

The back of The Shack was outdoors in the sand and if you wanted to go in, it was only polite to shower off!

Henry had a convenient shower to get rid of some of the sand, so she did just that, rinsing off from her knees to her toes. She felt the stress of the last few weeks dissipating a little bit. What could be wrong on the beach? Well, there were a million or so things wrong. Ali shook it off; her own negativity was just as annoying to her as it probably was to her sisters.

She slipped her flip-flops back on and wandered into the restaurant. At noon it was seat yourself, so she did. It was loud—so many tables filled with so many people. Well, *at least Henry's business is going well*, she thought.

She knew Henry would be here somewhere, but she didn't want to interrupt his busy day. She just wanted to sit, have someone feed her, look at the water, and watch other people enjoy the moment. Somehow, she'd forgotten how.

Ali picked a table toward the back that was empty and sat down. It would take a minute for someone to help her, which was fine. The waitresses looked very busy.

And then she saw him across the room.

She was struck again by how comfortable, casual, and handsome Henry was. It was kind of fun watching him in his element. He'd created the perfect beach restaurant. Now that she'd been working on The Sea Turtle for a while, she really appreciated what it took.

She watched Henry joke with some customers. Then a woman came up behind him, put her arms around his waist, and whispered in his ear. The woman looked very comfortable with the gesture, like she'd done it a million times before.

Ali sank down in her chair. Could she hide behind a napkin dispenser? Could she make herself invisible?

The woman kissed Henry's cheek and slid around to the front. Again, it struck her how natural it appeared for this woman, this beautiful, younger woman, to be cuddling with the guy who was supposed to be her boyfriend.

Ali realized, in that moment, that she was no smarter than she'd been last year, when she'd caught Ted in a similar scenario. Of course, Henry wasn't exclusive. Why would he be? And she'd given him nothing to indicate she was anything but a stressed out, middle-aged, Type A, overprotective, under-achieving, shrew.

Her opinion of herself shouldn't be impacted by Henry's love life. *Ugh.* But it was.

She needed to get out as fast as possible. She didn't want him to see her. Unfortunately, when she quickly stood up, she crashed into a server with a tray full of drinks.

The drinks fell to the floor all around her. She apologized to the server. It was awful. Everybody saw her—including Henry.

Ali wanted to shrink but couldn't, so instead, she decided to run. She ran out the back of the restaurant. If anyone called her name, she didn't hear it. Her ears felt hot, and they rang inside to her brain.

She should've gone left to go back to The Sea Turtle. Instead, she turned right. She didn't want to talk to anyone or see anyone.

She'd walk away from this scene, from the resort, from the mess that she couldn't clean up.

Was she destined to be cheated on? Destined to almost get her dreams only to see them crash around her at the last second?

Ali realized that all the things she thought she was building here had the permanence of a sandcastle in high tide.

# Twenty-Seven

## JOETTA

Didi inhaled as hard as she could. Despite the effort, the little blue balls wiggled and went only halfway up the plastic tube.

"One more time, come on."

Didi fixed Joetta with a death stare. But she complied with Joetta's request.

"Fine." Didi gave it a second go. This time the strength of her inhale produced a marginally better result.

"NICE!"

"Okay, if you keep talking to me like a child, I'm going come over there and smack you upside your perfectly coiffed bob."

"Such violent threats, you're clearly on the way to your old self again."

Didi laughed and then winced.

"Ooh, sorry." Joetta knew that the incision area was still painful for her sister.

Palmetto Ridge was the best step-down hospital in the area. Jorge was stubborn, but he hadn't argued with Joetta about this.

She'd insisted on footing the bill for whatever services their insurance didn't cover. Period. Of course, Didi didn't know that. If she did, that would be another reason she'd want to smack Joetta. Joetta didn't care. Didi would have the best, even if she was too stubborn to know how she got it.

"Enough about me, I hear you had a little luncheon."

"I did."

Didi clapped her hands together. Both were bruised from the multiple lines they'd poked into her. Right now, all her IVs were gone. This was huge. Didi was thrilled to no longer be a human pin cushion, as she'd called herself.

Joetta was visiting each morning and Jorge in the afternoon. They knew her rehab schedule, meals, and when she seemed to need to nap.

Didi continued to tell them both they did not need to babysit her, and they both continued to ignore her. "I know you both have important things to do. Let me do my work getting better without all the hovering."

"Nope," Jorge told her. And Joetta had been in total agreement with her brother-in-law, for once.

Now, Joetta told Didi about her recent contact with Faye and Blair. "I showed them that letter, the one Bruce wrote back on, with the threat."

"That man," Didi sighed. "I wish I'd have had my iPhone back then. I could have recorded him saying much worse."

"Well, that cuts both ways. You could have recorded me too, being awful, tipsy, chaotic, missing school drop off, falling down. That would be great too."

"You know forgiveness isn't going to be easy."

"Oh, I know. I'm going to keep saying sorry to the girls for the rest of my life. Even though both of them wanted me to stop. They are so amazing. How in the world did I not mess them up? Give it to Bruce, I guess."

"No, not *their* forgiveness, *yours*. You need to forgive yourself.

Stop looking at the worst moments you had with them. Stop berating yourself for living this life. You did make mistakes. We all did. But you're owning up to that. The girls will open up to you. I know it. But you have to stop hating yourself."

"I'm not the only one who hates me."

"Ali loves you. I watched her tender care of you so many times. It's still there."

Joetta squeezed her eyes shut. "I did the most damage to her. And I can't forgive it. She won't either. I don't deserve it."

"Joetta Armstrong, you are wrong. It's about time spent, and showing up. That's all you need to keep doing, and it's going to work out. Better than you can imagine."

"Look at you, Little Miss Sunshine of Palmetto Ridge!"

"I don't know about that. They asked me to fold laundry as some sort of rehab activity, and I told them to stick their detergent pod where the sun don't shine."

It was Joetta's turn to belly laugh, imagining that scene. She hoped her sister was right; she hoped that she could get her girls to forgive her.

"So, when are we coming clean to Banks?"

"Ugh, can you give me one second to process anything?" Joetta stood up and walked to the window.

Didi was going to recover. That was a guarantee, she knew now, because her big sister was pushing her to tell the truth, forgive herself, and tell Banks about the missing ten years she'd lied to him about.

Banks would hate her too. That was another guarantee. And the reason she continued to lie.

Lie. Lie. Lie.

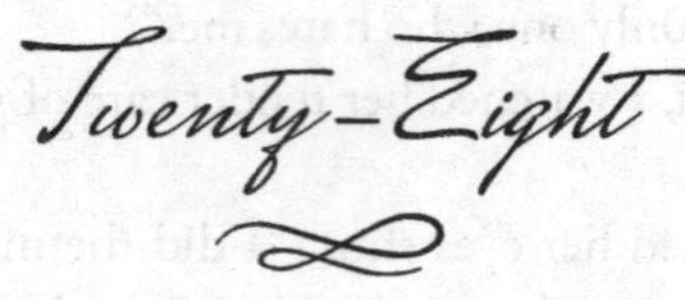



## ALI

She hid from Henry and his phone calls. He'd called at least a dozen times after her inelegant sprint from The Seashell Shack.

He really didn't need to say a word to her. She wasn't his wife, and honestly, she'd pushed him away as the financial reality pulled her under. She didn't want help, least of all from a guy who was, sadly, more like Ted than she'd recognized.

Henry even showed up on the property a few times, but Ali always scooted into her vehicle and drove off when she saw him walking on the beach toward The Sea Turtle.

It was time to be an adult though, and this time when her caller ID read *Henry*, she picked up. Ali planned to cross Henry off her to do list. Rip the band-aid off, as it were.

"You picked up! Ali. I need to explain. I know it looked bad but—"

At least he had more decency than Ted. Ted. The serial cheating that had happened under her nose. For years! *How dumb was I?* And of course, the handsome and charming Henry was playing the field too. He was a former baseball player, and she was just blind to the realities of life. Thus, the living in a beach resort thinking she could make this life work for her entire family. What a dangerous delusion she'd been living in.

Well, no more. She wasn't even mad at Henry, she just felt silly. Embarrassed. Old.

"Henry, you don't have to explain. We're not married. We're not even Facebook Official, as the kids say." She tried to sound light, fun, blithe, even cool! She felt none of those things.

"I need you to know that I do want to be exclusive, I *am* exclusive with you," Henry replied. "However that works for you."

"Uh, well, it doesn't. I'm sorry. Just not really ready. And I don't have any claim on you. Really. Just enjoy your life and all that. Okay. So, thank you for all the help you've given me here. I just really appreciate it."

"But—"

"I need to go. Okay, we're good. But you know, friends."

"Ali!"

"Goodbye." Ali ended the call.

She felt like a sixteen-year-old girl, one who was in the midst of full-on heart break. *What the heck?* Her divorce had fueled anger and determination. This? It just made her utterly sad.

But it was done. Henry knew she wasn't angry, so hopefully he's stop trying to string her along with whatever else he had going on. It was a string she didn't need as she made the hard decisions.

The next hard decision was waiting for her in a pink office in the little downtown of Haven Beach.

The offices of Patsy Gleaner Real Estate smelled as floral as the wallpaper on the walls.

Patsy had become a friend. Between Patsy, Erica Bell, and Henry, Ali had begun to feel like she'd made connections, bonds even, in this new place.

But they were temporary. This had been temporary too. A fever dream in the Florida sun.

She decided to meet with Patsy in her office so as not to risk being interrupted by anyone who would try to talk her out of this. This was the smart thing to do.

Patsy wore head-to-toe Lily Pulitzer. She looked like an ice cream cone in the best possible way.

Patsy hugged her in greeting and then sat down next to Ali in the two chairs that faced the glamorous glass top desk with gold accents. This entire office looked like jewelry, Ali decided. It was so perfectly Patsy.

"I'm going to sell. Well, *we* need to sell."

"The news from the engineers was awful, I take it."

"It was. We're looking at a million in repairs, before we can even begin to think about opening the Inn."

"Phew, that's a pretty penny for sure."

"Yeah, and you once told me if I sold, it could go for tens of millions. So, you know, that's what I want to do. It's what I have to do."

Patsy's lips tightened into a little line. "Here's the problem, we now know what needs to be done. So, the sale won't be as clear cut. We're going to have to disclose the report. That's one thing."

"I thought you said some developer might just want to tear it down and use the land for new condos? Really pack them in?"

"Yes, that's still possible. But honestly, the market is soft right now. It's been months since you told me no sale. Things are changing here. Across the state, really. The number we talked about isn't the number that's realistic."

"Great. Well, I can't afford a million in repairs, no chance."

"You know, let me make some calls. If you really want to sell, a deal could be out there."

"Just put up a sign and see what happens?"

"No, not exactly. I need to work on this a little. Okay?"

"Fine, but do me a favor? Let's not tell my sisters until it's all figured out."

"Honey, they're your partners, don't they need to be in the loop?"

"They don't, I don't want them to worry like I have been. They both have other things to deal with, and I want to have a plan in place so it's easy for them."

"You're sure about that?" asked Patsy.

"I am, it's just better if we iron this stuff out and then I'll let them know. Trust me. I got us all into this mess and I need to get us out."

"Okay, I'm the oldest daughter too. I get it. Take charge!"

"Right, yes."

"I sure will miss the Grand Finales though."

"Me too."

"On that note, I'm headed to visit Didi tomorrow. I hear she's almost back to her old self."

"She is, but that's another good reason to get this done. Didi and Jorge deserve to retire and stop worrying about that place."

"You're doing a lot of planning for other people's lives. Just saying."

"Which I plan to stop doing, once we solve our million-dollar problem. Okay?"

"You know you can count on me. Let me get some feelers out in the water!"

"Thank you, Patsy, you're a true friend."

"Also, a pink shark! Just what you need, girl."

Patsy winked and Ali felt slightly better. She'd fix this, all of this.

# Twenty-Nine

## BLAIR

She'd been on the phone and on email and even on Zoom. It wasn't easy to get a review removed. But it was very clear someone had it out for The Sea Turtle and that was easy to prove.

All the reviews had come in on the same day.

All the reviews were similarly phrased, and all of them were posted on every possible platform available to review a resort.

She collected screen shots, times, spelling errors, and sent it all up the chain at each site. Luckily, Blair had a very good friend who did marketing for The Cincinnatian Hotel, who had walked her through the process of dealing with spam reviews.

Within two days of the initial posting, Blair had made serious headway. Still, who was so spiteful that they'd slam The Sea Turtle? Blair had a few suspects. Obviously, there was Ted. Was he trying to sabotage the place out of spite, again?

In the end, Blair wound up getting all but two spam reviews removed. She showed Ali, and the two that remained were the legitimate experiences of two families.

One had been there when Ted was up to no good, the other had arrived when Ali first got to The Sea Turtle. She explained that there was no doubt that the pool was green slop that day.

Now the pool was an additional selling point. Though Blair knew they needed better photos of it, and the whole place. Actually, they needed a website, social media, and kick-butt listings on all the hotel and vacation sites.

She went to find Ali to outline all of it for her. As usual, she was doing something backbreaking without help.

"Ali, what the heck?" Ali was in the parking lot area, raking rocks. Actually raking rocks.

"We have a few divots here that need filled in. It's a five-thousand-dollar cost to have a gravel guy come out and redo the parking lot. That is NOT happening."

"Girl, you look like heck."

"Thanks."

While Blair was getting a little curvier, her skin literally looking glowy, and finally her hair had some bounce, Ali was wan. Her face was drawn, and her hair was in a ponytail with wispy and sad tendrils escaping a scrunchie that had seen better days.

"You could use a break. A bath. And a beauty salon."

"Um, I could also use a budget, so guess what, no beauty break for me." Ali had an edge to her voice. Normally her patient sister wasn't snappish.

"Sis. I'm kidding. Sort of. You're working yourself to death."

"No, I'm sorry. I'm just trying to save money and do stuff on my own."

"Last I checked you have Faye, me, Sawyer, and I think Katie would come back down given even one tiny hint that we could use her to work here. And how about Tye? He'd love a gig on the beach, who wouldn't?"

"No. Absolutely not. We have enough eggs in this basket, and this basket has a huge hole in it. Do not, under any circumstances, call my kids."

"Hey, okay, okay. Hey, look, this is good news. We're looking much better on the review sites."

"Good, but how to recover from the empty spots in the calendar where bookings used to be?"

"I'll work on that next. Meantime, do you want me to show you the plans for the marketing?"

Ali looked like the last thing she wanted to do was talk marketing. But it was better than raking rocks, in Blair's estimation.

"Do whatever you think, I trust you. Just don't spend any money."

"Okay, let's spend money on finding someone else to do this job here, you're going to hurt yourself."

"I'm fine. Now you get out of the sun and get a drink of water. Nugget is job one."

Ali's face softened when she talked about Blair's baby. That was something. It was something that made Ali happy even when she was eyebrows deep in whatever chore she felt she had to do alone.

Blair was about to do just that when a sharp pain shot through her. It felt like a vice had gripped her around the middle. She gasped and her legs buckled.

Ali was there at her side, helping her to the ground.

"What? What's wrong?"

"It hurts, I don't know. Something bad. We need to get to my doctor."

"On it. Don't move."

Ali ran to the office. Blair tried to get up off the ground, but another wave hit her.

"Can you walk?"

"I can try." With huge effort Blair stood up, leaning on Ali, and the two women made their way to Ali's SUV. Ali helped her climb in. A second after she sat down, another cramp shot through her.

Ali drove as fast as the law would allow to the OB's office. She reached out and let Blair hold her hand.

"Squeeze as hard as you need to, honey," Ali said.

They pulled into the parking lot, and Ali told her to stay put. "I'm getting a nurse and a wheelchair."

Blair didn't argue. Ali was out of the SUV in a flash. Blair's phone buzzed. She answered a text from Faye and then Joetta.

Then there they were: Ali, an orderly, and a wheelchair. Blair felt another wave of pain. This was a miscarriage; it had to be a miscarriage. Along with the pain there was panic and fear. What could she do to stop this? Did she cause it somehow?

She didn't really think she could get pregnant and then she was, and even with the worst circumstances, this little baby was helping her turn her life around.

The idea of losing it was too much. She wiped a tear away from her face and let them wheel her into the office.

Her OB was waiting.

They asked Ali to step out. They had an ultrasound machine and a stethoscope and a blood pressure cuff. Blair felt lightheaded now, like she was floating above herself.

This couldn't be happening. Whatever it was.

She really wanted her mom right now. And then things when gray.

*Thirty*

## FAYE

In the show *Three's Company*, when there was a mix up, a misunderstanding, a mistaken identity, hilarity ensued. Faye loved that show and watched endless reruns when she was a kid. Ali watched *Little House on the Prairie.*, but for Faye it was all, "Come and knock on our door..."

And now a colossal Kelly Girl mix up played out in the waiting room of Dr. Zabak, Blair's OBGYN.

While Blair was fighting for her baby's life, both Faye and Joetta showed up at the same time. And at that very moment, Ali walked out of the exam area to the waiting room to find them.

There was no laugh track, no prat falls, just an awkward silence as Ali processed what she was seeing.

Faye and Joetta had clasped hands when they'd entered the waiting room. It was unintentional, it was natural, and it just happened. Faye didn't even realize they were doing it. Faye and Joetta had reached out for each other as the nurse confirmed that Blair was indeed in the other room, in some sort of distress. It was how they managed their fear over the fate of Blair and the baby.

And it told Ali all she needed to know. Faye and Joetta had some sort of relationship.

Ali spit out a question, quiet, devasting, and worse than if she'd yelled it.

"What is *she* doing here?" Ali didn't acknowledge Joetta. She directed her anger straight to Faye.

Faye was about to answer when Joetta stepped forward.

"I texted Blair, she told me she needed me. So, I am here."

Ali again ignored Joetta.

"Our sister is being cared for by the doctor. I drove her here after she collapsed in the parking lot. She needs her sisters, a doctor, better hydration"—and now she finally locked eyes with Joetta—"but she does not and never has needed you."

Joetta didn't answer or fight back. She dropped Faye's hand. Faye's heart was racing. She felt caught, like she'd done something wrong. Was it wrong to spend time with their mother? Was it wrong to forgive? *No. It couldn't be.*

But it was wrong to lie. She'd lied. And so had Blair. They'd gone behind Ali's back and, despite years of absence, they'd discovered having Joetta in their lives was something wonderful. New, yes, uncertain, absolutely, but Faye and Blair saw a future where Joetta could be there, could be a part of their family.

"We've had a few chances to talk. I think you need to see the bigger picture. Mom, Joetta, has got a story to tell that we didn't know about."

"'Mom,' is it? Moms don't bolt. Are you forgetting that Mom pretended she was dead? Are you forgetting that Mom, when she was with us, was a raging alcoholic and couldn't be bothered to get sober for us?"

Joetta shuddered, the words seemingly hit her like little knives.

"She's right, Faye. I'll go. I don't belong here."

"Did Blair ask you to come?"

"Yes, but I should have realized. This is too much; I don't want to drive a wedge between you girls."

"Nothing you do can hurt me anymore, Joetta," Ali declared. "Nothing. Now why don't you do the one smart thing you've thought of since, oh, I don't know, the early '80s and get out of here so we can care for Blair."

Faye had never seen this side of Ali. She was like a wounded animal, attacking instead of letting anyone help her.

"Yes, I'm leaving."

At that moment, a nurse came out into the waiting room.

"She's calling for you," the nurse said.

"I'm coming," Ali replied.

"No, she's asking for her mom. And I can only let one of you back there, okay?"

"Go," Faye said.

Joetta tentatively stepped toward the nurse.

Ali was statue still. Her face was frozen.

Faye decided enough was enough with Ali. Yes, they'd been wrong to go behind her back, but Ali was wrong to think she could control everyone's relationship with Mom.

"Let's go out into the hall," Faye said.

"I do not want to—"

Faye interrupted her. "I don't care. You're not in charge right now. Let's go, big sister."

Ali did as Faye commanded. It was a gamble, but it had worked. The two women were now in a more private space.

"Why? Why, after all I told you, after you *promised*, did you bring that chaos into your life? She is going to disappoint you. She is going to hurt Blair. Mark my words."

"Ali Kelly, you listen to me. We know you were the worst hurt by Mom when she was with us. We know you remember things we don't, and even I do have a little. But she was forced to leave. You get it? FORCED."

"What?"

"Dad was a Grade A jerk to Mom. Yes, there was a drunken car crash. She freely admits that. Feels awful for it. And mind you, that's the last drop of booze she ever had. But Dad cut her off, told her not to come back. He threatened her."

"Come on, you believe that? As stern as Dad was, he never hit us, he wasn't violent. That's a line of bull she's spinning."

"Really? Think about what he said when he was dying. And more than that, I've seen proof."

Ali didn't reply to that, so Faye continued. "I've seen a letter she wrote, begging for him to let her have visitation, begging to do anything to come back into our lives. And Dad told her she'd be out on the street. That anything she built here would be ruined. I saw it. She had zero options."

This took the fire out of Ali, to some degree. She went from bitter to battered. "Look...I just feel so hurt. I feel like you both just ignored what I did to try to protect you from her. What I have done for decades to try to be there for us all."

"Ali, we love you for that. And we don't forget a moment. But if you close the door on whatever this is, well, you'll look just like Joetta. And cutting a person off for a mistake, that's Bruce Kelly's playbook. Just look at the damage that has caused all four of us."

"I'm not Dad."

"No, and you're not Joetta either, you're a combo platter. We all are. And we missed out on growing up with Mommy, but you know what, I don't want to miss out on anything else. And I can tell you that Blair feels the same. Why do you think she texted Joetta? She knew you were here."

"She wasn't in her right mind, I'm sure."

"I think she sweetly believed you'd put your own issues aside and focus on the fact that we all just want to be sure Blair is okay."

"I do want Blair to be okay, I—"

Ali was crying, and Faye couldn't stand it. She stepped forward and hugged her. Ali allowed herself to be hugged, but not for long.

"Let's go back in, let's find out how Blair is. We can sort this other stuff out after she's out of the woods."

"Fine, okay."

They collected themselves and inquired with the desk on their sister.

"You can both go in now." The nurse led them back.

They rushed to Blair and hugged her. Joetta was on a stool, in the corner. She seemed to be trying to be even smaller than her petite frame. Faye, too, felt sick to her stomach. *How had their sweet little family gone so sideways?*

And then the doctor came in.

"So, Blair is suffering from Toxemia. Her blood pressure was through the roof. And she can literally do zero, total bed rest, if she wants to keep this baby."

"OH! You didn't lose the baby!" Ali said and squeezed Blair's hand.

"No, the baby is okay. But momma here, she's off her feet for the duration. I'm assuming all three of you can care for her. I mean no food prep, no housework, no walks on the beach, no nothing."

Joetta stood up. "We will take care of her."

Ali stiffened; she clearly wanted to contradict Joetta. Faye watched as Ali did her very best to keep her mouth shut. Ultimately, Ali cared more about Blair's safety than her feud with Joetta. So, she stayed quiet. Faye was grateful for that.

But Faye had no doubt that whatever blow-up Ali was suppressing would eventually come out. She just hoped all three of them could make sure Blair, in her current state, was nowhere near the blast zone.

They had a little nugget to protect, and on that, all four women were united.

# *Thirty-One*

## JOETTA

These days, Joetta was going from waiting room to waiting room. No sooner did they have Blair settled than she needed to do the same for Didi. This was good news; her sister was cleared to go home! But Jorge and Didi needed help.

Joetta and Jorge helped Didi out of the car. Didi, for her part, tried to smack both of them away when they offered her a hand.

"I was released because I am strong enough to stand up. To get out of a car. To go to the little girl's room. All by myself, kay?"

Jorge bowed in deference to Didi, his queen.

But Belinda, aka Didi, was not Joetta's queen! She was her bossy big sister, and right now, she was being peak bossy.

"You fall and break a hip on the way up to the condo, let's see how fun it is to go to the little girl's room. Take Jorge's hand, you old bat."

Didi stuck out her tongue at Joetta, and Joetta rolled her eyes right back. There was a comfort in this back-and-forth. Didi was getting stronger. She'd finally been allowed home after weeks in the hospital and then the step-down.

Jorge insisted he could care for Didi, and Didi insisted that she didn't need anyone to care for her. Joetta tuned both of them out.

She'd contacted a private home healthcare company and scheduled a full-time nurse for the next two months. Both Jorge and Didi had objected to the idea, to the cost, to the very presence of someone in their condo.

And then both had quietly thanked her. For Joetta, the cost was nothing compared to the peace of mind she would have from knowing that both Jorge and Didi would be able to get stronger together.

The nurse's aide could do laundry, prepare meals, take Didi on walks, and generally give Jorge a chance to rest. Up until a few months ago, it was his health they were worrying about. The hot potato of aging didn't go away; it just got passed around.

Joetta was able to pay whatever it cost for one reason. And that was Banks.

Joetta had married very well that second time around. At the time, Didi was suspicious of her motives. Which was justified. Didi and Banks were friends. And Joetta was a mess, back then. But another pregnancy, the upheaval of her life in Toledo, and the stark reality that she needed to provide for a new set of children sent her running to Banks.

That was how it started. But she grew to love Banks; her childhood friend had turned into the love of her life. Banks never raised his voice, never said no, never questioned her with suspicion. And slowly over the years, his support helped her flourish. Joetta knew her worth in their community and in their family. She nearly stopped hating herself.

Nearly.

When she told Banks about wanting to hire a nurse's aide for Didi, Banks didn't blink.

"We need her up and at 'em, yes. Whatever you think is best."

Joetta had never had a real job. She provided support for Banks, made his life stylish, and made sure that his home, his clothes, and his life were on par with the country club he owned. Banks never once asked her to contribute financially. The opposite. He opened his heart and his wallet to whatever she needed.

And after her life with Bruce, she never took that for granted.

What would Banks say if he learned about the Kelly Girls? Her girls.

Joetta had been telling Banks she was at the hospital, and then the step-down and now, at Didi's home. She hadn't breathed a word of her daughters.

Joetta was a coward, straight up. If she told Banks, and he kicked her out, she'd be ill-equipped to survive.

Joetta calculated her time. She was coming up with viable alibis for where she'd been. The salon, the store, the aesthetician, the decorator, and on and on.

Despite Ali's objection, Joetta was going to help take care of Blair. Nothing could stop her from grabbing this second chance with her baby girl. But she also was in no way ready for Banks to know about it.

She would have to lie. She was good at lying. Maybe it was her one true talent.

Another element to her advantage? Banks was a creature of habit; she had exactly four more hours before he'd be home and wonder where she was.

Joetta just needed to be organized and meticulous for her lies to float undetected around her trusting husband.

The good news was that Didi was home. Jorge was taking a nap, so Joetta showed the nurse around.

She had time to go see her daughter.

She went into Didi's room one last time.

"You look tired. Time to sleep and stop being ornery," Joetta said and surveyed the room. Water by the bed, a box of tissues, the remote for the TV, and Didi's phone were all in easy reach.

"You look like you're up to something."

"I'm going to The Sea Turtle to spend time with Blair."

"That, baby sister, is music to my ears. What does Banks think about that?"

"You know very well he has zero clue. And I don't want him to, not now at least." *Not ever*, she thought, though how she was going to continue this juggling act, she did not know.

"You've never given that man enough credit."

"You're kidding, right? I owe him everything. He is everything. I don't give him credit?"

"Exactly, credit for being able to love you even the parts you've been hiding."

"I cannot talk about this right now." Joetta did not want to bring up the fact that it was Banks footing the bill for the nurse. She wasn't about to upset that apple cart when Didi was still in recovery. She also didn't want to fight with her sister.

"Let me amend that, you need to give yourself credit."

"Your oxygen to the brain is compromised, clearly, you're making zero sense."

"Those girls are forgiving you, and so will Banks, but you need to forgive you too."

"Sure, right. For now? Just focus on not dying, okay? I need you to not die and help me deal with those Kelly Sisters. The Gulfside Girls need to be full strength for who knows what's to come."

"I have a come-to-Jesus convo with Ali on the horizon. That much I know."

"Good luck, she's a tough nut." Ali had avoided Joetta, and when she did look her way, Joetta got the cold stare. Ali Kelly Harris was the toughest nut, and that was putting it mildly.

"Yeah, yeah, get out of here and give that little Blair a hug from her auntie."

"Fine. Yes."

Joetta kissed Didi on the forehead and headed out the door, with one more note.

"I'm sending Miss Cindy over here to do your hair. You're in need of a cut and color. It's criminal how bad that hair looks."

Didi shook her head at Joetta. It made Joetta smile, and a huge weight was lifting at least on that front. Didi was going to pull through. Joetta was not lying about that. She needed her big sister if she was going to figure out the next steps in this mess she'd made.

## Thirty-Two

ALI

Patsy had delivered. She called Ali and told her she had a solution. Ali hadn't breathed a word of it to her sisters.

Patsy was set to meet for lunch at The Morning Bell to lay out the plan. Ali hoped that it would leave all three of them in a better place.

After the scene with Joetta at Blair's doctor's office, Ali had remained separate from Faye and Blair. She'd gone to Moe's to stock Blair's cottage kitchen. She checked in several times a day, but she'd also run into Joetta doing the same thing, so now, she texted her sister before she popped in. Ali only went over to the cottage when she knew the coast was clear.

She was going to help Blair, but she would not be forgiving their mother.

Ever.

Meeting at The Morning Bell was also intentional. She didn't want her sisters to interfere with her plans to solve this problem and sell The Sea Turtle.

They didn't know the extent of the bill they were facing. Maybe, if things were normal, if there wasn't this distance between them, she'd have finally opened up. But as it stood, Faye and Blair were aligned against her with Joetta. Ali would never have predicted this situation. A mother returned from the dead, and her two sisters as distant as her ex-husband at this point.

Ali got to The Morning Bell first, and Erica clocked her right away.

"Hey, you!"

"Hey."

Erica came over. "Mind if I sit?"

"Of course not, I'm sorry I've not been around very much lately."

"Just so you know, Henry is about as sad a sack as I've seen, even worse than after his divorce."

"Uh, sad was not what I saw the other day." Ali had her armor up on all fronts.

"Girl, he told me you saw him get attacked by Sheila."

"Sheila?"

"Yeah, the woman is a total opportunist. She dated Henry, oh, what, maybe two months after his divorce? Huge mistake on his part, but he was a puppy singleton."

"So, they do have a thing. That's sure what it looked like."

"No, not at all. She's just a huge friggin' flirt. She acts like that with every man this side of Tampa."

Ali squirmed in her seat. "Look, we weren't even dating, much less exclusive. No harm, no foul."

Erica leveled a stare at Ali. "You're a liar."

"What?"

"You have the serious likes, if not loves, for Henry Hawkins, and he feels the same."

"Excuse me? I have a very bad detector for men who like to, let's just say, date around. That's Henry. Just like my ex. I do not need my heart broken or to be humiliated. Okay?"

"Henry isn't catting around. I'm telling you: you got it wrong. But I also get that you're very new to being out there. I'm not here to push you. But it's the first I've seen you since you broke our old baseball player's heart."

"I broke his heart?"

"Ya sure did. I forgive you. If you're not ready for a relationship, that's totally understandable. But if you are, and you're not dating Henry because you saw Sheila act a fool? Well. That's a shame. A big shame. He's a great man, and I'd like to see him happily ever after with a great woman."

"He'll find one."

"He did. You."

"You're a very good friend, and I'm so grateful to have met you. I just can't right now. There's a lot going on that I have to fix. And so yeah. Maybe I'm—what'd you call it? A puppy singleton. Tripping my way through it."

"I get it. I've been there." Erica gave her a warm smile. And then Patsy appeared at the table.

"Hello, Patsy! The usual for my favorite Florida Real Estate Diva?"

"Yes and make it a double! I have three showings this afternoon."

"You got it." Erica stood up and gave Ali's shoulder a little squeeze as she went back to running her darling little Morning Bell.

"Gosh, I hope you have good news."

"I do. It's not exactly what I told you when you first showed up in Haven Beach, thanks to the fact that we now know how much work needs to be done. But I have a deep pocket willing to take on the project and buy the property."

"That is great news."

Patsy outlined the deal. It wasn't life-changing money, but it was better than the debt that was about to drown them all.

Better by a mile.

Now to let her sisters know that they were getting out of the resort business. Seeing as she'd been the one leading the charge. They shouldn't be too tough to convince.

*Oh, who am I kidding? I have no idea what my sisters will do at this point!*

* * *

The next day, she arranged for Faye to meet her at Blair's cottage for breakfast. She had the details in place. And she was ready to make their day, if not their year.

"How are you feeling today?"

Blair was dutifully sitting on the deck of the cottage, looking at her computer.

"I'm bored in the cottage and I'm in the cottage bored."

Blair was singing a TikTok meme from back in the lockdown days. Ali wondered what it would have been like to survive that time here, at the cottages. She'd have to ask Didi. In fact, she and Didi had a lot to talk about. Least of which how they'd move forward with the Joetta of it all between them. Ali was all loose ends and messy family these days, and she hated it.

"Well, you've got a nice view at least." She tried to put a smile on her face and be upbeat. She was delivering good news.

"That is true."

Faye showed up a few minutes later with coffee from The Morning Bell and several croissants.

"Hey sisters!"

"Hey," Blair said.

"You want to give us your big news out here? Darn lovely morning," Faye said.

"Do you think we could plant something on the deck? Seeing as I'm in confinement here."

"I could, yes, you could watch them grow with your feet up."

"Yeah, yeah. I get it, total bed rest."

"Okay, so yeah, let's get to it," Ali said as Faye handed her the coffee.

While her sisters sat and waited for her to speak, Ali paced up and down the deck. Why was she hesitating? This was good news. This was the solution to her problems, all their problems.

"Are you here to say you've reconsidered your position on Mom?"

"Mom? Ugh, no, not at all. No, this is important."

Ali saw the look that shot between Faye and Blair.

"Okay, bad choice of words. I know you two have, uh, a relationship with that woman. I just have other things to deal with, and that's what we're going to talk about."

"Okay, shoot," Faye said.

It was weird to have her sisters' minds unknown to her. It had always felt like she could read their thoughts, and they hers.

"I'm selling The Sea Turtle."

The announcement was met with silence.

"Excuse me?" Blair asked.

"*Selling?* We just got here. What do you mean you're selling?"

"The repairs to The Sea Turtle Inn were more than I told you. Way more. A million dollars more."

"Whoa, you said it was manageable, that there were multiple bids, and that you had it handled. A million?"

"Yes, I didn't want you to worry. I didn't want you to know, honestly, that this whole thing isn't going to happen."

"So, what is it? That ten-million-dollar condo developer price tag we talked about in the beginning? We all agreed that we wanted to build something here, not sell out," Faye said.

"No, because of the work that needs to be done. However, a very deep pocket that Patsy Gleaner found, is willing to take on the whole thing, despite the fact that it could be condemned. Yeah, they may tear it down, but we won't have to do a thing. Just sell and we're out. Cash in hand."

"A deep pocket?" Blair asked.

"Yeah, someone wants the whole stretch of beach and is willing to pay us three million. After taxes and what we've put in, that will be a decent profit for each of us."

"But we've been over this. We don't want to sell. This is the dream job, building a great place for memories for families."

"Faye, we can't afford to do that. I don't have a million bucks to repair the Inn, do you?"

"Can't we get a loan or something?" Blair asked.

"You're about to be a single mom," Ali told her, then turned to Faye, "You're retired with, let's face it, a fixed income. And I've blown through my divorce settlement and the money from Dad trying to make this work the last six months. I'm trying not to throw good money after bad."

Faye stood up and squared her shoulders. "Ali Kelly. I have had just about enough of you making decisions for the three of us."

"What? You're the ones who pushed me to make a go of this. I knew it was a risk. I didn't make a decision for all three of us."

"Since the moment Mom came back into our lives, you've been telling us what to do. Not to talk to Mom, not to help with the resort. Plus, you've kept all of this about the Inn to yourself, and generally been, well, a real pain!"

"Excuse me for trying to protect you, like I've done my entire life." Ali felt the sting of tears in her eyes and the sting of her sister's words even worse.

"How can we do this together if you don't share anything with us?" Faye said.

"And we aren't kids anymore, Ali," Blair added. "You do not need to stand in for Mom or anyone else." Blair's words were soft, while Faye was hot right now.

Ali could count on one hand the times her sisters and she had fought; the last time was something about who could use the car they shared in high school.

"Be that as it may, this place is going to be sold. If you don't sign off, I'll call a lawyer and force the issue."

"Ali, sit down. It's time you learned a little more about how we got here."

"I know how we got here, through the lies of our parents. I'm trying to untangle us all from that. This place is full of lies, that's what I've learned."

"No, it's not, it's full of sand, sun, and fun. Blair, where's the box?"

"In the bedroom next to my nightstand."

"What is she talking about?"

"You'll see."

Faye walked into the cottage and then back out. She gave Ali a shoebox filled with papers.

"Read on, and then we'll talk," Faye said.

"Come on, Blair, we're going to sit by the pool while our big sister has her world rocked," Faye said and put her hand out to Blair. "We'll be back in an hour or so."

With that, her two sisters left. Ali felt stung. They were going to make this so much harder than it needed to be.

She looked at the box.

It was a shoebox, the brand was one she recognized but had never worn, Etienne Aigner. *More evidence of Joetta's high-end taste?* She carefully opened up the lid even though the taste right now in her mouth was bitter.

Stacks and stacks of letters were piled neatly in the box. Would letters from the past rock her world? Ali doubted it.

She was there, she remembered Joetta as a mother.

Everything Joetta did was a lesson to her own mothering style. Despite her job, she'd never missed a play or a practice or a conference.

Whatever the letters revealed couldn't change the fact that

Joetta had missed it all. Ali inhaled in an effort to find some sort of calm, and the smell nearly knocked her over.

It was faint, but the letters were perfumed, the perfume her mother used to wear.

Revlon, Charlie. Mommy used to mist it in the air and let the girls run through the droplets. They were the chicest-smelling children at Old Orchard Elementary.

*Fine, Faye*, thought Ali. *You win; I'll read the letters....*

*Thirty-Three*

## LETTERS FROM JOETTA

*Dear Bruce,*

*I had to leave Toledo. I had nowhere to stay, and you've made it so I can't get into the bank accounts. I can't pay for a hotel.*

*I just wanted to tell you that right off, so that you know that is why I am not sitting outside of the house trying to get in. Didi is letting me stay with her at her apartment in Florida. I have a court date on the docket. I will be back in town for that. Please let me see the girls when I am there.*

*I also want you to know I have entered a program. I am not drinking ever again. I promise you. As I have said over and over, I am so sorry. I know it is not enough, and I only left because I have nowhere to stay. Again, I will be back for my court date. I can come early. I can stay. Please let me see the girls at least.*

. . .

*Love, Joetta*

* * *

*Dear Bruce,*

*All I can say is I'm sorry. It is unforgivable. Please answer the phone. Please tell me where you've taken the girls. I went over to your mother's house. She wouldn't answer the door either.*

*I know what I did was horrifying. I know we could've lost everything. Please figure this out. I will be a better mother, a better wife. I will do anything you ask.*

*I understand what I did put the girls in danger, but I promise I will never drink again. I promise I will do whatever you ask me to do. Please let me see the girls. If you can't forgive me, let me still be their mother.*

*Love, Joetta*

*Dear Bruce,*

*I've got a great idea. You know that place my family has? If we tried to start again at The Sea Turtle, it would be neutral territory. I meant there—you know it's beautiful. We wouldn't have to pay for any lodging. It would be a chance to reset things, to try again. What do you think?*

*Love, Joetta*

• • •

Dear Bruce,

I received probation from the City of Toledo because no one was injured, and it was my first offense. I suppose I got off easy. All I can do now is try to be a better person. I've attached the legal filing, so you can verify that I am telling the truth. I know you don't trust me. I understand that.

Let me say again—I have not had a drink since that awful night. I can't imagine what the girls think. Please let me just see my daughters.

Love, Joetta

Bruce,

I've contacted an attorney. There is no way you can do this. A judge has to decide, not you. Please do not make this decision. Let's work this out. Here's my new phone number. Please call me.

Joetta

Bruce,

I am giving the resort to the girls. The documentation is enclosed with this letter. I am doing this, so they know that even though you won't let me see them, they mean everything to me. I'm hoping this will show you—and them—that even if you don't want to see me, I am still their mother.

The property will be held in trust until they are adults. Although I don't have any money to give, this will be more than enough over *the years to hopefully support whatever you need for them. I have signed the papers; they are enclosed.*

*I understand that you never want to see me again, but I am their mother, and Blair specifically needs me. Have some compassion. She is a baby, if you don't let me see her, she won't even remember me. I can't believe you're this cruel. I know you're not.*

*Don't do this. Please let me at least have visitation. I'll leave everything here in Florida and get an apartment in Old Orchard. I'll wait tables. I do not need anything but the girls.*


*Joetta*


Ali counted one hundred letters, give or take, all pleading for Bruce to change his mind. One from Didi, even, and an AA Sponsor, and all written in a flurry over a few weeks.

Joetta had tried. Ali could see that, feel it.

She attempted to put herself in Joetta's place. She remembered how fragile her mother had seemed to be back then. Not like the slick package she was today. She was a summer society baby dropped into Bruce's blue-collar beer life.

Maybe she could see, just a little anyway, how much Joetta wanted to be with them. It hurt her to read and to feel how raw each letter was.

Finally, Ali got to the bottom of the pile.

The last letter was on letterhead from a notebook. It was fat-lined. Ali recognized it as something she'd have had in a Trapper Keeper. Her dad had grabbed a sheet of paper from her notebook to write the next devastating missive.


*Joetta,*

·  ·  ·

*Here are all your letters. I do not want evidence of you here. You are making this more difficult than it already is.*

*I have written down my conditions. If you continue to harass us, I will call the Haven Beach Daily Register's society page. The reporter, Jackie Pillsbury, was very interested in any scandal about the Bennett and Armstrong families.*

*Just in case you think I am bluffing, I have enclosed a copy of your mug shot.*

*I am certain your new life—your parents and your new husband—would be very ashamed, as am I, of your behavior.*

*If you would like to continue to live without everyone knowing how terrible of a mother you are, stop immediately. Forever.*

## Bruce Kelly

Ali thought about Bruce. She remembered the formidable man he was, not the shrunken elderly one she'd cared for at the end of his life.

Everyone in the house did what he ordered. He was a Marine, a union boss, a throwback to a 1950s ethos, and someone who did not suffer fools.

Joetta was no fool, but she was dying there, in Toledo, in that house. Ali knew more now about addiction. She used to think her mother could just stop drinking and all would be well. Joetta had a profound problem, though, and Bruce was ill-equipped to deal with it.

His solution, cutting Joetta out of their lives, telling them she was dead, seemed right to him then. But even he, as he lay dying, knew it was wrong. He knew he'd sinned against them, even more than her careless moment behind the wheel.

Ali had blocked out every memory she had of Joetta as a good mother. She'd done it to protect her heart from the devastation. She'd been the caretaker of her sisters before their mother died.

*Ugh, not died, left. And not left, at least, not willingly. Maybe I should think of it using a new word.*

Her mother didn't die, but she also didn't leave. Her mother was banished.

Ali thought back, and this time, a warm memory bubbled to the surface. One she hadn't thought of in over forty years.

## Thirty-Four

1981

Ali

"Shh, don't tell your sisters, or it'll be a melee!"

Ali would not mess this up. She was quiet and scooted under the covers with her mommy. The TV was on low, and there was popcorn in a bowl between them.

Daddy was hunting with his friend Uncle Butchie. That meant Mommy was in charge, which also meant Ali had made lunch and dinner for her sisters.

But now, in the middle of the night, Mommy had quietly woken her up and told her to come to her parents' room.

Ali and Mommy watched *Saturday Night Live*, as Eddie Murphy pretended to be Gumby. Ali had no idea who Gumby even was, but watching her mother lose her breath from laughing so hard made Ali laugh, too.

Ali and Mommy watched the whole show. Ali must have fallen asleep, and her mommy must have taken her back to her own bed.

When she woke up, she was in her room. But she knew she'd gotten a special treat, just her and Mommy.

# Thirty-Five

## PRESENT DAY
Joetta

As she drove to The Sea Turtle, there was a distinct feeling that she might be sick or pass out or maybe just turn and run.

After over thirty-five years of no drinking, she really could use one right now. Take the edge off. Stop feeling all of the things.

After thirty-five years of sobriety, she also knew this was a time to touch base with her sponsor.

"Siri, call Caliope."

Caliope Windsor was her current sponsor; she was two decades younger than Joetta. And she was Joetta's third sponsor over the years.

Joetta was also a sponsor for others in the program. She'd even led meetings at various times in her life.

It was key to the program, the ability to call someone who knew. The opportunity to externalize the emotions and urges and get through them without a drink.

Banks knew she was in AA, on that she'd never lied. But

mostly, the only thing he really knew was that if Joetta got stressed, her sponsors were there to help her talk through it.

"Hey Ann Taylor, what's shaking?" Caliope answered right away. Caliope thought Joetta looked like she should be a pint-sized Ann Taylor model, and the nickname had stuck.

"I'm feeling that old feeling right now."

"Any reason?"

"Not a mystery, I'm about to make amends to some people who were hurt the most by my disease."

"Ah, hair of the old dog, old tricks. You really don't need me to tell you. Say it out loud, Ann Taylor."

"I need to feel the feelings. Feeling bad is a part of life. Sit with it. Let it be."

"And then?"

"Let it go. Not sure if I can do that last one."

"You already won, you know that, by calling for help."

"I do know and thank you."

"No need to say that, go forth, Ann Taylor, into whatever Preppy Handbook scenario you're headed into."

"Will do."

"And ma'am, do not sleep on a meeting this week, *especially* this week."

"Right you are, as usual."

"Good luck, Joetta, you'll be okay."

They ended the call.

Another call had prompted this journey. Of all people, Ali had called her. It was a terse call. Adult Ali was always all business. So was little kid Ali.

She was a Type A problem-solving Oldest Daughter dealing with a perennial cadre of Baby Sisters. That had to be a challenge!

The last time Joetta had been face-to-face with her eldest daughter, it had been devastating. All the hurt she'd caused her kids. All the chaos she'd caused Ali specifically, when Ali was just a child. All of that was on Ali's face.

Faye and Blair had so few memories of her; maybe that was the only reason they could open their hearts now.

Ali knew. Ali saw who she really was, more than even Didi or Banks. Ali knew.

Joetta had put up a brick wall as best as she could when it came to memories about her time in Toledo. It was the only way she could survive after it was clear that Bruce would rather destroy her than allow her to be with the girls.

But since that moment in Didi's hospital room, Joetta's wall had been crumbling in chunks. She felt raw and exposed in a way she had always feared. In a way, she'd guarded against it, since she knew it would force her to accept the impossible.

Ali said all three girls would be at The Sea Turtle, waiting. They all wanted to talk to her. Maybe Ali had convinced her sisters that it was a terrible idea to forgive Joetta?

*Maybe it was.*

As she drove to The Sea Turtle, she remembered her cute little kitchen in Old Orchard, Toledo, Ohio.

# Thirty-Six

## 1984
### Joetta

She didn't cook very often. When she and Bruce had first married, she did try to fix meals, to be a good wife. Bruce didn't like what she knew how to make. She argued that if you bought good ingredients, you'd be satisfied with less food. So, there was no difference in the budget.

That was wrong. Bruce insisted on a vat of Hamburger Helper or a pile of macaroni and cheese. He wanted quantity.

But on Bruce's birthday, so long ago, she'd tried her very best to make a meal worthy of her husband. He loved something called potato soup, of all things. To her it was heavy and mushy, but Bruce loved it.

Her mother-in-law knew how to make it and, in fact, was the only one who could make it to Bruce's specifications. In preparation for the birthday dinner, Joetta had sat at the hands of her mother-in-law and learned exactly how to do it. She wrote down every step, and as she stirred the concoction, she hoped it would be up to snuff.

The ingredients were simple—potatoes, flour, milk, salt, pepper, and onion—but they had to be combined in a certain way.

Joetta had spent the afternoon first shopping and then cooking. By the time Bruce got home, she had it all ready. She'd even added a little extra, some ground beef, which he liked in his Hamburger Helper. Now this was a meal!

She had the girls help her set the table.

Ali was so cute. She was a mini-adult and really always had been. Ali congratulated and encouraged her mother as though Joetta was the one in elementary school. It was so charming. *Someday, Ali will be such a good mommy*, Joetta thought.

When Bruce got home, he was in a mood. True, he was never one to whistle a happy tune or brightly yell, "Honey, I'm home!" But today it was worse than usual. He stomped into the kitchen and roughly placed his lunch pail on the counter. Joetta, however, was determined that they were going to have a good dinner for his birthday, and that was all there was to it.

Joetta ignored Bruce's surly demeanor. She offered to clean his lunch pail and pack it for the next day.

"Sure, you will. The last time you promised me to do that, you put something stupid in there."

She'd packed him a Caesar Salad. That was what Bruce considered "rabbit food."

Joetta wouldn't let him ruin his own birthday.

"I promise I will do a good job of it for tomorrow. Change clothes and come back down. The girls and I have a big surprise for you."

Despite his mood, Bruce did as she told him. He looked fresh and clean and still so handsome when he reappeared. That handsome thing had left her with three kids and all alone at the same time.

Bruce sat at the table. She put the soup in a bowl in front of him.

"What is this?"

"Potato soup."

"What's in it?"

"Well, you always said we have to have a meat and a potato, and the soup doesn't have meat, so I added a special twist."

"This is disgusting." Bruce stood up, took his bowl to the sink, and dumped it inside.

The girls started to cry. This time, he was ruining it, not her, for a change.

"See you in a few hours. I'm going out to the shed. Got some work to do."

"But the girls want to celebrate your birthday. They made cards."

Bruce walked over to the mantel.

"Thanks, kids," he murmured, but still stalked out of the house.

He was always at work, or in the workshop, or at the union hall, or even on his dad's fishing boat. They never seemed to be together, like they had for that brief time when they'd met on the beach.

*Maybe that was it. Maybe they should take a vacation together to a beach somewhere?*

Joetta sat at the table. She put a piece of bread on baby Blair's highchair tray. She looked at the flowers that Faye had arranged in a little vase and had carefully placed in the center of the table. They were mostly dandelions, but they were beautiful.

"Well, girls, let us have dinner. It looks okay, doesn't it?"

She didn't know what to do. *Should I make them eat the disgusting soup?*

"Mommy, it tastes wonderful. Don't you think it tastes great?" Ali had started eating the moment Joetta suggested it.

*What a sweet little soul, trying to salvage the dinner.*

"It's true," Faye said, after Ali kicked her, very unsubtly, under the table. "It's great, Mommy."

She watched her two girls eat the defective soup as if they were all together celebrating Bruce's birthday. She was so grateful for how sweet her daughters were.

But the truth was, she'd failed. Again.

Bruce was in the garage doing some sort of chore rather than sitting with them and appreciating what they'd tried to do for his birthday.

Joetta poured a little vodka in her water glass, careful not to let the girls see.

It helped.

## Thirty-Seven

**PRESENT DAY**

Ali

They gathered at the Blueberry Bungalow. Ali and Faye had helped, but really, Blair had made it her own. It was decorated with adorable little blue cottage touches.

Ali hated pulling the rug out from under her sisters, but they'd all have enough with the sale to be set up very comfortably, somewhere else.

Ali had to face a different reality now. It was her turn to face Joetta.

Ali realized that she could no longer hang on to the anger about their mother—that it was hurting her as much as it was hurting her mom. She thought back to Bruce's final days, the things he had said.

"*I did it to keep you three safe,*" he'd whispered in his final moments.

She remembered the words that made so much more sense now.

*"You understand? I am sorry, but it was bad. You could have died."*

He'd said he needed her to know. He'd said he was sorry.

*"I tried to do the best. But I'm not her. I couldn't be her."*

She knew now what he was apologizing for. She would tell Joetta these things. And other things he'd said in his final moments. Bruce's regret was Joetta.

She closed her eyes tightly at the memory...

*"I had the best three daughters."*

Everyone in the situation thought they were doing what was best for the girls—for her and for her little baby sisters. In the end, the hurt that it caused couldn't be undone. They couldn't change the past, but they could affect the future.

Ali didn't know what a relationship with Joetta would look like, but she was willing, at least, to try—or at least to not get in the way of Faye and Blair.

There was a light knock at the door, and she jumped up to open it.

"Come on in."

Joetta Armstrong looked terrified. Ali felt terrified. She realized this meeting would go whichever way she wanted it to go, so she thought she'd plunge right in with honesty.

"I'm not sure if I can ever forgive you."

Joetta looked like she'd been slapped.

*Yikes,* Ali thought. That wasn't exactly the right way to start. It wasn't exactly what she meant, either, so she tried again.

"I guess I should say that differently. I'm not sure if I can ever forgive you—but I am going to try."

With that, Joetta sucked in a gulp of air like she'd just breached the surface after diving underwater.

Was that what her mother felt?

Faye stood up and went over to Joetta. "We gave her the letters."

Joetta shook her head, no. "I shouldn't be forgiven. I did the worst thing. I just thought it was the right thing. He told me it was the only thing. Every year, I tried—for years and years—just to know what was happening in your lives, Ali."

"Just so you know," Ali said, "one of the last things Bruce ever said before he died was that he was sorry."

"That *he* was sorry?"

"I didn't know what he was talking about, but he struggled, in his literal last breath, to tell me, to apologize."

"I guess there was a lot of that going around," Joetta said softly. "For what it's worth, I've never had another drink. I want you to know that."

"That's worth a lot," Ali said.

"What can I do?"

"Just give me time. I see now that you didn't just leave. I see now that you weren't the only one lying. I know my dad was a tough person. He was stubborn. He was intractable—all of those things."

"That's why I gave you this place. I knew he wouldn't. I was trying so hard to do something. Most of what I did back then was wrong. The fact that you three are such amazing women—I'm just so grateful. I was such a screwup."

It was strange to see this woman, who looked so put together, fall completely apart. Ali remembered this dynamic. Her mother was delicate. This Joetta had seemed strong, powerful even. But the fragile woman she remembered was still there.

"I'm so sorry. I don't want to be forgiven. I just—I don't deserve it."

"Everyone deserves it," Ali told her. "And I'm sorry too."
*Sorry that I have so much of Dad in me.*
This was going to be a long and difficult process— forgiveness.

Ali stood. She walked across the room. She put out her hands. Joetta looked at her in awe. They were exactly the same height. Joetta put her hands in Ali's. The same hands, too.

"I remember when it was just you and me," Ali said.

"I do too, sweet little girl."

"I'm not such a sweet grown-up," Ali said.

"You're an amazing woman."

"Well, it sounds like you are, too. You're not the same person who crashed that car, or who left us."

Joetta moved her mouth to speak, but no words came.

Ali stepped forward and pulled Joetta in for a hug.

This was her mother.

This was the best part of her mother.

Hopefully, this was the part that Ali could love.

## Thirty-Eight

## FAYE

It was almost too much to process, this new era of their lives. So much had changed.

The processing part made Faye realize that Blair needed to rest. If Faye's blood pressure was any indication, all of this was not good for the total bed rest plan Blair was on.

"You, lie down, glass of water, feet up," Faye said, and the three women fussed over Blair until she was cocooned in bed.

"Bed rest is stupid," Blair said. "I mean, I need to get out on the beach WITH you!"

"Ask for a prescription for the Grand Finale from your doctor; only then will we allow it," Ali said.

The three women decided the only way Blair would get to rest was if they left.

But they unwilling to just part ways. If Joetta left, would she come back? That was the unspoken mistrust they all had from their childhood.

"We'll bring you back a treat," Faye promised Blair.

Ali, Faye, and Joetta walked out of the cottage and toward the ocean. There was a familiarity now to Joetta that Faye was so happy to feel, to see. Ali, removing the wall, had also removed the brittleness in Joetta.

"You should've seen your aunt back in the day," Joetta said. "She had the cutest white bikini. I was always jealous of her curves."

"So, you met Dad right here?"

"Yes, I did. And as much as we were talking about the past, he was handsome—and in the beginning, we were in love."

Faye liked to hear that. Faye loved their father, warts and all. They all did. They didn't want to cast him as the bad guy, but he was the reason they hadn't seen their mother. She'd made the mistake, but he'd made her pay a terrible price.

"I have a question. Dad never had the answer," Faye said. "Who named us?"

"Well, that was on me," Joetta said. "Your dad said that he would name the boys, and I would name the girls. So, as you can see, I got that job three times. Ali, you're named after Ali McGraw," Joetta said.

Ali laughed.

"Yes! I saw *Love Story*, and I was so into that movie. She was so beautiful, so stylish. So, when you came along, Ali just popped into my head."

"All right, Faye—that's an easy one," Faye said.

"Yeah, I'm not so mysterious in the naming department. Faye Dunaway in *Bonnie and Clyde*. I saw that movie and realized I had never heard a more beautiful name than Faye, so there you go, Faye."

They continued to walk as the water chased up and down the shore.

"I can't believe it's been so long since I've been here. Your aunt and I used to spend every single day we could out at the beach. My parents used to say that this part of Haven Beach was slumming it. Look at these multi-million-dollar homes! This was literally the budget section."

"Were your parents awfully strict?" Ali asked.

"Oh, they were. They didn't want me to *talk* to your dad—much less date him! They threatened to cut me off. When I found out I was pregnant, we ran. It sounded so *Bonnie and Clyde*, so *Love Story*. I took a lot of jewelry and clothes, and Didi gave me her jewelry too. That was my little nest egg."

"You know, we found most of that stuff? Dad never threw it away."

"Really? Wouldn't mind seeing some of it. It's been a long time."

"Well, some of it wound up on eBay, but some of it we still have," Ali said.

"Honestly, Ali is the only person who could really fit into any of that stuff. You guys are both the same size. It's amazing," Faye said.

And it was amazing how much the two looked like each other. All of a sudden, Ali's face—which had been deeply lined with worry lately—looked a lot less so. Both Ali and Joetta looked younger. The weight of their relationship somehow had gotten lighter in the last hour or two.

"What about Blair? Where did that come from?" Faye asked.

"The *Facts of Life*?" Ali asked.

"No, there was an actress. I think she's still around—Blair Brown. I thought, 'What a pretty name.' Blair Brown."

"You sure liked your movies and TV," Faye said.

"I did. Also, I hated my name. What the heck is that? Joetta? I was looking toward movie stars to find glamorous names for you girls."

"Well, in an era where everyone was named Jennifer or Ashley, you did help us stand out," Faye said.

"Good."

They walked for a good hour, and when it was time to get a snack at the Seashell Shack, Ali begged off.

"You guys go ahead. I have some work to do with the sale of the resort."

"What? Sale?"

"I've had enough dramatic scenes for one day, and I do have a lot of work to do. So, I'll let Faye fill you in, uh, Mom. Okay, that feels weird. Maybe a little too soon for that, Joetta. Yeah, sorry, that will have to do for now."

Ali had reached her limit with bonding time. That was fair. And it was big news, selling the resort. Faye would have to explain, even though she wasn't on board at all. She also didn't have a solution to the million-dollar problem.

Ali said her goodbyes.

Joetta and Faye went into the Shack as Ali went back to The Sea Turtle.

"She's selling The Sea Turtle."

"How can that be? It's been in the family for literal generations!"

"Yeah. Turns out the bill for the repairs, which you have to do—"

"—Oh, the new regs are just terrible, though I heard they may loosen some of them, down the road."

"Well, regardless, it's a million-dollar bill we can't pay."

"But we've had The Sea Turtle in the family for seventy years." That phrase was bittersweet: *in our family...*

"I know. It's a bummer. But she's got a good buyer, and, well, one thing about Ali—like she said—she's just as stubborn as Dad when she wants to be."

"I can't believe we're going to sell The Sea Turtle."

"Well, no one I know has an extra million dollars sitting around, so right now that looks like what's gonna happen."

Faye hated the idea of selling The Sea Turtle just as much as

Joetta seemed to. The lightness of the reconciliation between Ali and Joetta was marred by the realization that their dream of running the resort was dying.

## Thirty-Nine

BLAIR

Blair was already tired of the bed rest directive, and she had months and months to go before this nugget made an appearance.

She was feeling stir crazy, useless around The Sea Turtle, and now, with The Sea Turtle on the market, she was feeling pressure.

Ali was being logical. Practical even. Selling this place and getting what they could out of it was smart. Operation Good Mom required Blair to abandon pie-in-the-sky dreams of living on the beach and start looking for a sensible house with a good school district.

Still, as she looked outside her front window, with the surf framed by palm trees, she knew she'd never be as happy in any other place.

A friendly face entered her framed view.

"Knock, knock!"

Ford was at the door with a treat and a smile.

"Come in!"

Blair struggled a bit to get up from her perch on the couch.

"No, don't get up. I've come bearing fruit from Moe's."

"That's too kind! I realize I'm eating for two, but the amount of treats you and my sisters are bringing, it's like there's a family of four or something in here."

Ford laughed and got to integrating his gift into her little kitchen. He knew she wasn't supposed to be on her feet and was sweet enough to be sure to not make work with his food offering.

"I'm sure that's not true, and I promise, I just did fruit. Gotta keep the blood sugar in check for The Nugget."

Somehow, everyone she knew had taken to calling her bump The Nugget. She was half convinced it would come out looking like an actual chicken nugget.

"Well, we had a big day today, even though I didn't move from this spot."

"Do tell." Ford was her first friend in Haven Beach, and in short order, he'd become her best friend.

Blair told the strange tale of the long-lost mother and how Ali took a huge step toward forgiveness.

"Yeah, I mean, I don't think we're all going to be wearing matching white blouses for a photo sesh on the beach anytime soon, but I no longer have to sneak around and lie to spend time with my mom."

"That's progress."

"It's so weird to say the words 'My mom.' I never had one, so yeah, just strange."

"And soon to be Nana Nuggie."

Blair laughed at that image; somehow, Joetta, with her perfectly coiffed hair and size zero Pulitzer wardrobe, didn't seem like a Nana. Maybe a Gigi?

"Yeah, so that's the good news."

"Which implies some bad news. Are you okay? Should I get your blood pressure cuff?"

"Yes, I'm fine, and I took it a little while ago. No, the bad news is the finances here. My sister has decided to sell because the cost of running The Sea Turtle just isn't sustainable with the upgrades that are needed."

"I thought you three were equal partners?"

"We are, and Faye and I technically could come up with an alternate plan, or you know, a million bucks. Hand me my purse over there by the table, I think I have a million in that one, next to my Altoids."

"You know, I could help with this."

"Spare million?"

"Uh, actually, spare couple of million."

As her friend explained exactly who he was and how he could help, Blair's blood pressure did go up.

## JOETTA

Joetta called their financial advisor. It was possible, even workable. She had access to the funds, but she did need one more signature for that amount.

Would she have told Banks, eventually? She believed she would. If Joetta was truly going to be in the girls' lives, she couldn't lie anymore to Banks.

Truth be told, of the twelve-step program that she lived by with AA, she'd never completed all the steps.

She'd lied to Banks to get him to marry her. He said he loved her unconditionally.

She believed she loved him unconditionally—but the conditions had been pretty easy for the last few decades. What if the waters were choppy?

She was about to be the storm.

She decided to rip off the band-aid that had been securely in place for forty years.

Joetta did not want the love of her life to be the price she paid to have the girls back. But liars and schemers didn't get off Scot-free. She'd given up her girls for Banks. Now she would give up Banks for her girls if she had to.

Banks was tan and looked very rested. His nephew was helping more and more at the club. It was good, and it was so Banks and Joetta could enjoy more time together. Joetta was about to blow all of that up. She prayed Banks would forgive her, but she also knew whatever his reaction, she deserved it.

She loved him in blue; he was wearing a blue golf shirt and shorts. It was hard to believe he was in his late sixties. He looked ten years younger at least, and without the benefit of her plastic surgeon. Men. That was so unfair. He looked at her with love; she relished it. Maybe it was the last time.

"So, I've got something to tell you."

"Bad news about Didi?"

"No. It's all good there. She hasn't driven off the nurse. And she took a little walk around their complex today."

"She's strong! I'm going to get her on the links by the end of the year, mark my words."

"I don't doubt it."

"So, the bad news?"

"The bad news is...well. I'm a liar." She just said it. She was a liar. A huge, awful liar.

"Honey, listen. I know you get Botox. It's fine. I know that the chandelier in the foyer was fifteen grand. Saw the bill myself. I forgive you."

"No, it's none of that." She wasn't smiling; she was barely able to hold in her tears. But she steeled herself. This wasn't a play for sympathy; it was accountability. It was a long overdue reckoning.

Banks stopped joking when he looked at her and realized she was serious. That she did have something bigger than a fifteen-thousand-dollar chandelier or a Botox bill to disclose.

"You know when we reconnected? When I came back into town all those years ago?"

"I do. I'll never forget that. You were sitting in the sunroom with your sister—I thought my dreams had come true. My ship had come in. There was the Joetta of my dreams."

"OK, you're not making this easy."

"What is it?"

*This is the last chance to pull the plug! The last chance to have him look at you and not hate you....*

Joetta ripped off the band-aid.

"So...my time away. It wasn't what I said."

She had lived the lie so long, she almost believed that she had spent a decade in her late teens and early twenties gallivanting through Europe.

She hadn't.

"When I left here...do you remember that boy everyone hated because he was kind of..."

"Not a country club type like us?" Banks was kidding, but also not.

He lived a snobby life but wasn't a snob. He'd been raised by elitists and owned the toniest club in the county, but he had a light touch, an open heart.

Joetta was terrified she was going to do damage to his good heart, to him, by revealing her true self. She nodded.

"Right. I do remember. Do I ever. I was so jealous of that guy!"

Joetta thought back to the Banks she'd grown up with. He'd had a crush on her, forever, and she'd ignored it. She'd taken it for granted, and she'd hurt him when she left. But he didn't even register with her selfish teenage self. She was so ashamed of the person she was then, and now.

Joetta pushed ahead; there was no denying the truth. Her three girls were here, and they had opened the window to a relationship. And it might all fall apart, but the truth was, she had to tell him. If she had a chance at being their mom again, she couldn't do it in secret or with lies.

And she owed Banks the full story.

So, she spoke it, out loud, for the first time to anyone but Didi. "That guy was Bruce. Bruce Kelly. And I was in love with him. Not like I'm in love with you kind of love—like immature, my-parents-didn't-like-him, kind of love. And I got pregnant. And my parents kicked me out. And I ran away. I didn't go to Europe."

And here was the big, bad, scary part. Banks sat silently; he knew her enough to know she was in the middle of the story, not the end.

"I had three children with him. I lived with him for a decade."

She explained a little bit about her life. About how she was ill-equipped to be a stay-at-home mom on a shoestring budget.

How she turned to alcohol to cope. It all seemed weak; she was so weak. Joetta struggled to have sympathy for her younger self.

The way she'd become the worst version of herself shouldn't be laid at Bruce's feet either.

She didn't blame Bruce for her failures as a mother or for her alcoholism. That was her, not him.

Banks interrupted. He listened. His face changed. But he didn't yell at her. He didn't castigate her.

But he didn't know the worst.

"And then, with my three girls in the car, I got behind the wheel, drunk. And we crashed. I crashed."

"My God, the girls, did they...?" Banks couldn't even finish the sentence. It was too awful to think about.

Joetta didn't divert her attention or the telling of her past to gauge Banks's emotions. "No, they were okay. I was in jail. Bruce wanted nothing to do with me. He took the girls. Didi came and helped me with the legal stuff."

"I really don't understand where this is going. Didi lied too. I just cannot believe I had no idea."

"I met you after Bruce told me to leave. I was trying to show him I was going to AA. I was promising everything I could think of, but well, he did not, would not, let me see the girls."

"That wasn't legal; you should have gotten a custody agreement."

There was Banks, trying to fix her issues for her, in retrospect.

"He insisted I sign a quickie divorce. So, I did. I thought if I did what he wanted, I could see the girls or salvage something."

"This was all happening when we reconnected?"

"You saved me, you know that, but even more than you realize."

"I still can't believe you'd allow anyone to take your kids like that."

"He told me that if I attempted to see the kids, he'd tell you, tell the papers here, that I nearly killed them. I was horrified. And also, I believed he was right. I was a terrible mother."

Banks paced back and forth in the kitchen. She couldn't imagine what he was thinking. His wife was not the person he thought, not by a mile.

"I can't process this. Three children. How could you?"

"Yeah, I will never forgive myself, I can't ever. But I can help them now. I deeded The Sea Turtle to them, back then, in an attempt to lure Bruce and the girls here. After he refused, I thought, well, let it be an inheritance or something. Didi sort of took it over after we married and life moved in new directions."

"Why now, why are you telling me this? Why didn't you tell me before? I don't even know what to do with this, with you."

"I'm telling you now because I need your signature."

"What the hell are you talking about?"

"I'm giving my daughters, who are now back in my life, the money to fix The Sea Turtle so they can run it as a resort and don't have to sell it. I have a tentative relationship with them, and they're in a pickle, and I'm going to help them out of it."

"So, three adults you haven't seen since, what, the mid-'80s, children of a husband who treated you badly, are telling you they're your daughters and they want money? That is out of the question. You're being scammed, and even though I am about as—

I don't even know what, angry or duped or whatever with this, I don't know—but I do know you're not giving these people money."

Joetta was totally unsure of her relationship status with Banks, and if he left her now, she wouldn't be surprised. But she was completely sure of her course of action when it came to the Kelly Sisters.

"I love you. I will spend the rest of my life trying to prove I am worth loving back. But there is one thing I know for sure. These are my daughters. And I am going to fight for them and help them any way I can. Until the day I die. I have a second chance with them, and I have to take it. I have to."

She walked over to her purse, took out the file folder, and slid it to Banks.

"Sign this or I'll be calling the financial advisor to cash in a different account, maybe my 401K. It doesn't matter even if I am living out on the street, Banks. I'm doing it."

Joetta knew she'd likely ruined the best thing she ever had. A good man. A perfect life with him. All of it was on the edge of a cliff, and she was kicking it.

She would pay that price. Joetta could do something for Ali, Faye, and Blair, finally, after all this time. And she wasn't going to be swayed or bullied or pushed into a different direction.

Her future was as the mother of the Kelly Sisters.

# Forty-One

## ALI

The contract was in her inbox. Ali was supposed to accept the offer by the end of the week. It was Friday morning. She only had one set of guests but darn it if she wasn't going to have a terrific Grand Finale, as it might be her last one.

She read the terms. They'd get three million for the entire operation. After fees, taxes, and paying off the credit cards she'd maxed to fund the last few weeks, well, that would be enough for all three Kelly Sisters to start over.

None of them wanted to leave Haven Beach, least of all Ali. But they'd all need to figure out their next act on their own. Faye at the Mangrove Garden Grotto as the hottest floral designer in the county. Blair, doing her remote marketing job and becoming a mother. And Ali...

Ali had no idea what her next act was. She had thought she was a good project manager. She believed herself to be perfectly cut out for the hospitality industry. But she had been so wrong about all of it.

What was next? She didn't really know. Haven Beach and The Sea Turtle had given her a purpose. She thought it would be forever, but instead it had barely been a year.

She'd have a little cushion, but it was a cushion. It would give her some time to figure things out. But she really was at a loss.

What did you do if your dream job was a bust? How did you move on if you were terrible at the thing you wanted to do most of all?

All questions she'd have to answer after she e-signed this deal.

Ali went to sign, and her phone buzzed. It was Blair. Her two sisters would also have to sign, as they owned a third. She needed to quit dragging her feet so they could just get it done and move on.

Maybe The Sea Turtle had done what it was intended to do; it had brought Joetta back into their lives. It had brought a secret out into the light. It had changed their family, hopefully for the better, forever.

Patsy said the resort was very likely to be torn down. This felt so wrong. The cottages were so beautiful, quirky, and perfect, and yet still affordable. Katie's cute ideas for the Inn would never be realized, either.

Ali really wished it wouldn't be torn down, but then beggars couldn't be choosers, as they said. She'd have a lot to do after they signed. She hoped she could get her kids down one last time before they moved on, and she'd have to call all the guests that Blair had rebooked to tell them the news.

Blair had fixed the bogus reviews. Ali still no idea who hated them that much, but she had a few likely suspects. And Blair had sold packages one at a time. Man, her sister was good at sales and marketing. That was a comfort. Her little sister would land on her feet, her and The Nugget together.

She read Blair's text:

*Come on down to the Blueberry.*

It was to all three of them. Three of them. That included Joetta.

The text sounded casual, but with her sister's recent health scare, Ali wasn't taking any chances. They still had hours before the end of business. She'd sign the agreement after she checked in on her baby sister.

When she got there, Faye and Joetta were also walking up at the same time.

"Everything okay?" Joetta said, her face worried, as they all were about Blair and The Nugget.

"I'm fine! Come in!" Blair yelled for them, and they did as she asked.

"It seems like all our family meetings are now at the Blueberry Bungalow," Faye said. "But I'm glad you texted. I was about to do the same. I have a proposal for all of you. This is going to make it easier. I can tell you all at once."

"Funny, I have great news, too, can I share it first?" Blair asked. She had, in fact, called this impromptu meeting.

"Ah, as long as no one's dying, we need to sign the sales agreement and then I've got a fantastic Grand Finale for us. Who knows how many more we'll have, you know?" Ali said.

"I think we're going to have as many as we want. I've come up with the money," Blair said.

"What?"

"Yep, you know my friend, the one who saved my keister when I passed out on the beach?"

"Yes," Faye said.

"Well, he's loaded. His name is Ford Taylor."

"The guy that owns the mansion over there?" Ali asked.

"The very same. He said he'd totally love to invest in The Sea Turtle, and let us run it, and has no interest in tearing it down. We could fix the Inn, and then he'd be a silent partner."

Ali didn't know what to think. She didn't know Blair's friend, but Blair was clearly super excited about her announcement. Ali was proud of her for taking the initiative but a silent partner? There were way too many possible pitfalls. She could see that Blair was very proud of coming up with the idea though. She didn't want to crush it.

"Well, okay, but I also have a solution!" This time, Faye spoke up.

"You're also dating a billionaire?" Ali quipped.

"Ford and I are just friends," Blair said.

Ali gave her a little side eye.

"What?"

"Hey, listen, middle child has the floor. Rudy and I want to turn the Inn and the cottages into a wedding venue. He'll co-sign a loan with me to do the repairs, and then we'll book events. I'll do the flowers; he'll expand his business interests in Haven Beach. No need to pay him back, we pay the bank. I'll get the loan, so we're really not adding a partner. We put the agreement in a fixed time period, you know. Not that the billionaire silent but deadly partner plan isn't great, but I'm saying there's another option."

Ali's head was spinning. A week ago, they'd had zero prospects of scraping together the mountain of money they'd need to keep The Sea Turtle, and now, in one afternoon, both her sisters had figured out solutions. She wasn't sure either was viable, but it warmed her heart and actually lifted her spirits. She'd shouldered this on her own for too long. And here were Faye and Blair with ideas and action.

"I don't even know what to say, you guys, that's just so amazing. I mean, Rudy, wow. I thought he was a plant guy, not a finance guy, but wow."

"Oh, he got into the plants after selling his tech firm, come to find out," Faye said and shrugged.

"Ha, well, looks like you two are way better at picking significant others than I am. Ted tried to sabotage this place, and these two guys want to rescue us from our financial problems," Ali said.

"We don't need a famous billionaire or a tech CEO," Joetta said.

Her posture was straight, and her voice was strong. So much so that Ali took new notice of her.

She was dressed in shorts, and her hair was a little looser than they'd seen before, in a cute way. She just had on some lip gloss instead of a full face of glam. Something was up with Joetta. *She actually looks younger, less done up*, Ali thought.

"I'm giving you three the money to fix the Inn," Joetta announced. "No more, no less. Ali showed me the estimate from the engineering firm. I am covering it. I don't want a stake or a silent or loud partnership. I have it. I'm paying it."

The Kelly Sisters looked at her, and no one said a word.

"Close your mouths, you'll catch flies," Joetta said.

"Mom, this is not your mess to clean up," Ali said.

"This isn't a mess; it is a business that was dropped into your lap out of nowhere. Of course there are hidden costs you didn't anticipate. I'm here to tell you that this place was my gift to you, mine and Didi's gift. And we want it to stay with the Gulfside Girls, which you three are now a part of. No man, no millionaire, just The Gulfside Girls."

Ali could hardly believe what had just unfolded in the last few minutes.

"Did you tell Banks?" Faye asked.

"I did. It's my money, mostly, and he's mostly not talking to me right now. But either he'll get over it or not. You're my daughters, and I have a chance, after all this time, to help you. I want to do it. I need to do it."

"We could keep this place, Ali. Think about it, just us three," Faye said.

"I mean, sure, I come up with a great idea and you two trump it, but hey, I'll find another way to use Ford's money," Blair joked.

*It was probably better for her long-term friendship with Ford if she didn't owe him a million bucks*, Ali thought. *Actually, it would be better if none of us owed a bunch of men a bunch of money.*

"I can't accept all this, it's too much," Ali said.

"Ali Kelly, you're not alone. Every problem isn't yours to solve, and if you'd have shared the burden a little earlier, we'd have solved it with you a little sooner. You didn't need to be the big sister on this," Faye said.

"You're a lot like Didi," Joetta said. Ali realized that was probably true, the nature of the beast, of the big sister role.

"I was so worried, I thought I'd really messed this up. I'd dragged you all here, and then it was going to go up in smoke." Ali nearly sank to the ground, and Faye came to her side, and then Joetta. Blair stood up slowly, mindful of The Nugget.

They surrounded Ali in a hug. They were there for her, even after she'd closed herself off and tried to manage everything on her own.

"We are all here for the long haul, even Mom," Blair said.

"Even Mom," Ali repeated.

It was more than she could have dreamed, her sisters, and now her mother. Here.

She hoped somewhere Bruce could see them and know they also forgave him.

## Forty-Two

### ALI

Ali enjoyed getting the wine, selecting items for a charcuterie, and even paying Sawyer to help her arrange the chairs in the cabanas. It felt like the first few days of her visits to The Sea Turtle. It felt like they had a future there, at last.

But before she went back to the beach to set everything up, Ali had a loose end to tie up.

Didi was Aunt Belinda.

Didi was a part of the web of lies Joetta had spun, but Ali felt Didi was caught in that web as much as Ali had been.

Ali had made a big stride with Joetta.

She allowed a good memory to surface, and once she did, other good memories blossomed. Good memories made it too hard to lose her mother; now that her mother was back, Ali took in the full breadth of their childhood, good and bad.

She'd avoided any real conversations with Didi when Didi was in the throes of recovery. This was out of deference to Jorge and because she didn't want to make anything worse as Didi fought for her life. But it was time.

Ali wanted the grand finale to be perfect. And she'd heard Didi had been on the fence about coming.

If it was because she wasn't strong enough, that was one thing. But if it was because Didi thought Ali harbored resentment over the past, that was something else.

Joetta and Ali's relationship was on a more truthful path; it was old and new at the same time. Ali and Didi needed to be in that same place.

Ali rang the bell at the condo. Jorge answered the door and gave her a raised eyebrow.

"So, I'm assuming I don't have to have any worries about this conversation you want to have with Didi?"

"I don't think you have to have any worries. I've learned a lot about how life doesn't go as you plan and how sometimes a lie isn't meant to hurt but meant to protect."

Jorge nodded; he'd been through the wringer over the last year. He wanted peace, and so did Ali.

"Look, it wouldn't be a Grand Finale without the grande dame."

"Very true. All right; she's in her room."

Ali walked through the little condo to find Didi in bed, but looking so much better than she had in the last few weeks. She had a lovely new haircut, matching loungewear, and, best of all, a rosy glow on her cheeks.

"So, you've come to lay it all on the line, have you?"

"I don't know. I guess I've come to make sure you know I understand."

"We're both the oldest daughters. I think we both understand each other more than any of these baby sisters."

"That's true. When I think about what I would do for Faye and Blair, it's not hard to see why you did what you did."

Didi started to cry. It was quiet, gentle even. Ali took a few steps closer and then sat at the edge of her bed. The two big sisters held hands.

"I just didn't know what else to do. You know, I came to visit you."

"I sort of remember that," said Ali.

"You were very responsible. It's one of the first times I saw that Joetta had a real problem. She broke a glass, and you cleaned it up. You were a child. You were put in the position to be the mother. I know it's hard to give up that role when your babies no longer need you to wipe up the broken glass."

"My sisters aren't my babies—that's another lesson."

"I'm sorry that I lied to you. I was just so excited that you were at The Sea Turtle. Other than the dreams I've had for my own kids, the dreams I've had for Joetta and the three of you—kept me going back to The Sea Turtle, hoping someday...."

"Listen, I can't say that I'm not going to drop a snide comment or that I'm over everything. It's still so mind-boggling. But I will say this—as far as I'm concerned, you and I are good."

"That's good, because I could kick the bucket anytime. I'd hate to have you mad at me when I go."

"Oh, stop. I heard your heart is working like a well-oiled machine."

"They say I'm still weak, but before you know it, I'll be walking up and down Haven Beach."

"Good. I want you in fine form when we have your beachside retirement party."

"Retirement?"

"Yes, it's time for you and Jorge to be officially retired. The door is always open, and the lounges are exactly where you left them. But the Kelly Sisters need to do the heavy lifting now, with an assist from Sawyer."

"In my book, that makes you Gulfside Girls, just like Joetta and me. And I'll tell you retirement sounds pretty good."

"I'll see you tonight at the Grand Finale."

"I wouldn't want to be anywhere else in the world."

"I'm glad. And I'm also glad that we are actually related. I felt like you were my aunt even before I knew you were."

Didi smiled.

"I tell ya; forgiveness works better than Botox on my forehead wrinkles."

"Agree!"

## Forty-Three

## GRAND FINALE
Ali

For the first time in months, Ali felt lighter. The sisters, as a unit, decided the best solution for The Sea Turtle's structural issues was Joetta's.

Ali did have some doubts. She'd gone from completely closed off to allowing Joetta to save the day. But Joetta had risked her comfortable life with Banks Armstrong to help them keep The Sea Turtle. That meant something.

She thought back to some of the memories that had been playing in her mind since they'd found out Joetta was alive. So many of the memories were sad or traumatic or involved Ali being an adult. She used to think she was forced into that because of Joetta's disease, but now she wondered if it was just in her nature to want to shoulder the burden for her family, all alone.

She'd done it here, and she almost lost the resort because of it.

The resort! The idea that she could keep pursuing this dream had lit her soul on fire! Her old optimism returned, and so many ideas popped into her head about how to make this place magical. Strike that, more magical. The sunset alone made it dreamy!

She'd spent the day getting ready for the Grand Finale instead of dreading the sale of their little piece of heaven.

They didn't have very many guests, just one family, but preparing for the Grand Finale tonight was different. She'd even sent out a text—a feeler, a sideways apology—to Henry.

She had no reason to think he'd show up. In the haze of her tunnel vision, when she thought she was the only one who could do anything, she'd also cut off Henry.

Sawyer had arrived two hours ago, and she was thrilled she could actually pay him to set up chairs and help her go get the food and just be the most awesome nephew ever.

"The beach looks rippin'!"

She assumed that was twenty-something-speak for good.

"It does! Could you go get those little plastic champagne glasses in the shed?"

"Sure thing. No problem."

Sawyer helped her put together what she hoped was a Grand Finale worthy of Didi.

Didi and Jorge were coming to the Grand Finale tonight. If Ali could forgive Joetta, she could forgive Didi. After all, maybe her instinct to protect, the Big Sister gene, came straight from Didi.

Ali looked out onto the water, and before everyone got there, she decided she would get her toes in the sand. She'd been so busy, so stressed, that she hadn't allowed the greatest thing about The Sea Turtle to do its magic.

She'd also been avoiding all the kaftans that Didi had given her. She decided, in honor of Joetta and in honor of this party, she was gonna do it. She selected a bright peach kaftan with coral sequins at the V-neck and pearl buttons down the back. It was gorgeous. And anybody who had been on this beach in the 1970s would have thought she was Joetta.

Ali had come to terms with that, too. She was her mother's daughter, and their mother deserved forgiveness.

She let the breeze blow through her hair, and she felt some of the stress of the last few months evaporate. She inhaled the sea salt air and exhaled the drama.

"That's a pretty snazzy outfit."

She opened her eyes and looked—and there was Henry. She meant to give him a proper apology. She meant to be cool. She had to try to explain herself, to tentatively why she thought what she saw was Henry playing the field, and why she wasn't going to accept that or ignore it ever again.

When Henry walked up barefoot, gray hair, sexy smile, and open heart, she decided—well, she didn't decide anything. She ran toward Henry, gave him a hug, and kissed him full on the mouth.

"I kind of like it when fights end this way," he said.

"Was that it? We had a fight?"

"Not even that. An unfortunate misunderstanding."

"I'm sorry. I judged you by a standard that I got used to with Ted."

"I get it. I just wish you had let me explain."

"Yeah, explain. You don't have to explain. Love means never having to explain."

"Well, well, well—I love you too."

*I just told this man I love him?! Who even am I?*

Ali laughed. She put her hand in Henry's hand, her head on Henry's shoulder.

They walked the beach for the few minutes before the Grand Finale would be in full swing.

*Forty-Four*

## FAYE

Faye was in charge of cheese and crackers.

"Wow, this thing is sliding all over the place," she said while driving the truck, trying to keep them from sailing off the tray. When they got to the parking lot of The Sea Turtle, it was more of a cracker pile than an arranged tray.

"Yikes, you are bad at that job," said Rudy.

"I really am," Faye laughed.

They liked working together, despite the cracker disaster currently headed toward the Grand Finale. They'd come up with a good idea about making The Sea Turtle a wedding venue—but instead of getting a business loan to make it happen, they decided to work with Ali's scheduling of bookings, to find out where the natural ebb and flow of business was. They'd use the wedding idea to smooth out the dips in income when it wasn't peak vacation season.

Faye was kind of amazed that Rudy was willing to jump into almost any business idea. She had never been in business, but he said she had a natural instinct—not only for flowers, but also for working with customers.

Since they had the money to fix up the Inn, Faye was going to move into the cottage next to Blair to be there for emergencies.

They could once again afford to live in the cottages while the Inn was being repaired.

This would be Rudy's first Grand Finale. He said he was a little nervous since her son Sawyer was going to be there. Her sisters had also taken to calling Rudy her boyfriend, so he'd best be prepared for some snarky sister energy!

She was dating Rudy Palm Tree.

She was setting up a burgeoning floral business.

And she was one-third owner of The Sea Turtle Resort. Getting laid off from the plant might have been the best thing that ever happened to Faye.

*Forty-Five*

## BLAIR

"I'm not an invalid. I can walk," Blair said.

Despite that, Sawyer was sent to bring his aunt slowly to the beach. It was only a few steps away from her cottage to the little spot they enjoyed for the Grand Finale party, but no one was taking any chances with Blair these days.

She had considered inviting Ford but decided against it. She felt bad rejecting Ford's generous offer, but in the end, she felt proud of herself for being able to come up with something as an alternative to Ali. Even though they'd ultimately gone a different way.

Ali had always saved the day, signed the permission slip, and wiped her tears. She saw now why having Joetta there was the hardest on Ali. And Blair also saw how the healing would take the longest between Ali and Joetta.

But it was happening.

Joetta was invited to the Grand Finale, and she was bringing Jorge and Didi.

They'd also have a couple of guests who were booked into the cottages!

"Not a bad turnout," Blair said as they approached the gathering.

"Here you go, Aunt Blair! You have to sit here, and I got a stool for your feet," said Sawyer.

"I'm not—"

"—Listen, I don't argue with Aunt Ali. It's not a good business plan."

"Tell me about it," Blair said. "How's school?"

"Oh my gosh, it's great. Gonna be in an art show in a couple weeks."

"Oh wow."

"Can I get lemonade for you? Water? Fruit punch?"

"That's a lot of selections. I'm fine for now, kiddo," she said.

Sawyer was summoned by a guest with a question, and he floppy-haired it over to help. Blair smiled. She hoped her own nugget was as amazing as her nieces and nephews.

"Speaking of Ali..."

Blair looked out to the beach and saw her sister kissing the handsome restaurateur of Haven Beach.

"Well, it looks like somebody's over Ted Harris. Looks like someone went fishing."

It was Faye and Rudy, bearing cheese.

It made her laugh.

Blair's problems weren't over just because they'd saved The Sea Turtle. She knew that. She'd changed her cell phone number, and her personal protection order against Blake was in place, but still, he was out there.

She had a little nugget. That little nugget was her top priority.

That meant keeping a secret from Blake as long as she could. She noticed her ankles were a little bit swollen, so she did as Sawyer recommended. She put her feet up on the stool.

No matter what her worries about Blake or Ali or Joetta, Blair knew a good mom took care of herself first.

## Forty-Six

## JOETTA

To Joetta's surprise, taking care of Didi meant Jorge was doing a better job taking care of himself! He was getting rehab and even making meals for them both. He seemed to relish not being the "sick one" for a change.

When he climbed in and out of Joetta's car, he didn't even make the old-man-getting-up-out-of-the-car noise.

"Jorge, you're gonna be dancing in no time," she quipped.

"I know. Footloose and fancy free over here," he said.

Joetta laughed.

Didi was moving a little bit slower, but she looked amazing. This was one of her first outings other than for doctor's appointments since she'd been released.

Jorge walked ahead of them, and Didi held on to Joetta's arm.

"Can you believe this place?" Didi asked.

"I can't believe it. I can't believe that it worked. That we gave the place to the girls, that we were able to save it."

"Pretty good trick, that. So where are you and Mr. Man?"

"I haven't heard from Banks. Of course, that worries me."

"He's staying at the club, I'd assume," Didi asked. They had several hotel-style rooms at the country club.

"Well, after I told him the big news and that I was going to use this money whether he liked it or not, he was pretty quiet. Silent treatment, actually. We've passed at the office, at the house too, but no connection. No forgiveness. I really don't know what will happen there."

"You did the right thing."

"I hope so. I mean, I know I did when it comes to the Kelly Sisters, just the lying. He may never trust me again."

"What about the rest of the story?" Didi said under her breath.

"I think the rest of the story would be the final straw."

"The truth is better than lying. You just learned that."

"I've done about enough learning for one week. Could you lay off?"

"All right, all right. I don't want to rain on anyone's happy ending, and this is a pretty happy ending."

"It sure is," Joetta said.

They walked through the pathways of The Sea Turtle until the space opened up to the little courtyard where her three daughters and various guests mingled and enjoyed the scenery and the sand.

Joetta had never seen Sawyer in person. Her grandson. She looked around for him.

Meanwhile, assorted guests swarmed around Didi and insisted she plop down next to Blair.

There were hugs and kisses. Joetta hadn't thought Didi was going to make it out of the hospital at one point. To see her back out on the beach they grew up on, filled her heart to the point of bursting.

At one point, Ali, sunlit, slightly bronzed, toasted everyone.

Faye, who was arm in arm with Sawyer, approached Joetta.

"This is my son, Sawyer."

"Hello. I like your hair."

The blonde, floppy hair reminded her of a surfer long ago.

"Thanks. My mom always wants me to cut it."

"Well, I think it's just right the way it is," she smiled.

"Thanks. Can I call you Grandma?"

"You certainly can—whatever you'd like."

"Well, Grandma...she doesn't have to go by Grandma," Faye pointed out. "She's allowed to pick a grandma name. That's what happens these days, you get to pick! Like Gigi or Fifi or whatever cool thing you want!"

"Oh, sorry, sure, what will it be?" Sawyer asked her and laid on her an adorably handsome smile.

Joetta laughed. "You know, Grandma sounds just fine."

*Forty-Seven*

# 1986
## Joetta

Joetta counted on the truth to sell her lie. Twin pregnancies rarely went full term. Of course, she had no idea she was pregnant when Bruce Kelly kicked her out. But she was certain of the fact by the time Banks Armstrong walked back into her life.

She calculated that she was only one month along when Banks caught her eye. Joetta's mind was now razor sharp without alcohol dulling her senses. She'd need every lick of brain power she had to keep construct her new life.

But honestly, it wasn't difficult to orchestrate a whirlwind courtship and wedding. Banks loved her. Well, to be more accurate, Banks loved the parts of her she showed him.

Joetta was likely six weeks along by the time she and Banks wed. She had to be meticulous. Luckily, Banks trusted her and, more than anything, wanted to believe she was a good person.

She told Banks she was pregnant one month after their honeymoon in St. Thomas.

"I can't tell you how happy you've made me. This is a miracle!" Banks hugged her and immediately gave her a credit card to outfit the nursery. He was so excited. The guilt Joetta carried like a stone on her heart got heavier. But she wouldn't unburden herself by telling the truth. The guilt was part of her penance.

At first, she was panicked at how big she'd gotten, so fast. How did 4-weeks discrepancy cause her belly to be that big? She worried, had she miscalculated? Was she further along than she'd guessed?

The ultrasound proved to be one of the most exciting moments of their early marriage.

"Twins!" Banks cried, and Joetta did too. Twins would be her explanation for everything.

This news also swayed her in-laws off the fence of skepticism and into her camp. Everyone was thrilled that two little Armstrongs were on the way. Twins.

Joetta used the twin pregnancy as the solution for any math that didn't add up. *She was big for only 5 months along! Well, there were two little bundles in there!*

She was nine months along when she went into labor, but everyone except Didi believed she was going "early." Twins, of course, often come early.

When the first contraction came, she had already rehearsed her lines. She'd said it to herself enough to make it as true as possible.

She walked into Bank's study and delivered it.

"It looks like the twins are going to come a little early." Banks looked up from whatever paperwork he was studying. His jaw dropped open.

"Now? Really?" She nodded. And then he ran to their room to get her bag. He loaded it into the car, then ran back to take her arm. Memories of Ali, Faye, and Blair flooded her mind. She'd done this before but couldn't reveal that. Ever.

Her previous deliveries were by the book. No major issues. This delivery was not. They pulled into the emergency entrance, and Banks ran around to her side of the car. As Joetta exited the car, she felt a sudden searing pain. It was a sharp stabbing pain, not the cramp of a contraction. This was different. This was wrong.

She felt a rush and looked down and knew she was bleeding. A lot.

Banks yelled for the orderlies. Something shifted inside of her.

"This isn't the normal way. This is not what it is supposed to be!" She breathlessly said these words to Banks and the nurses now bundling her onto a gurney. Later, she wondered if Banks thought that was a strange thing to say. How would she know what was normal?

But Banks was so worried for her and the babies that it likely passed him by. She was sedated, and Banks was there. She mumbled things. She forgot any plans or rehearsed lines. She was so scared for her babies.

And then, she was unconscious.

She woke up in the recovery room with no idea on how much time had passed. She looked around the room. She found two sweet baby bundles, one in Banks' arms, the other in an incubator.

"Banks, are they okay?"

"Oh, they're just perfect, two perfect little girls. This princess is just in need of some warmth. They're surprisingly robust for how early and how much trouble you had. You scared the heck out of me."

Banks leaned over and kissed her. She peered at the baby in his arms.

"I want to hold them." Banks transferred the baby in his arms to hers. So beautiful, her head was covered in dark hair. Then Banks brought the other baby to her, this angel had downy white hair on her head.

"Salt and pepper, eh?" Banks smiled, and he was also crying. She tried to adjust in bed and felt pressure in her abdomen.

"What, what's wrong? Why can't I move? Did they do a C-section?" Banks' face turned very serious. He seemed to be looking for the right words.

"Honey, the doctor said you had a uterine rupture. They had to give you a hysterectomy; it was the only way with the bleeding."

"Oh, my," Joetta didn't know what that meant, but she remembered the sharp pain and the bleeding.

"I'm so sorry, I just couldn't lose you. And our family is perfect now as long as you're okay. We're all okay."

"I'm the one who's sorry. I didn't mean to scare you."

"I love you, Joetta. Now you need to rest and let me watch over the little babies."

"That sounds good."

Joetta was tired, she gave the baby back to Banks and watched as he carefully adjusted them in their little bassinettes.

Joetta thought back to her previous deliveries. Bruce wasn't in the room with her when she had her girls. This was so different.

Banks was talking to nurses, pulling the little ski caps around their ears, fussing over her covers and water glass.

She wasn't going to have any more children. She was so lucky to have these two, and she could give them to Banks.

He could never know.

She thought of names and as before, her favorite movie stars were her inspiration.

"Jessica and Jamie, those are the names. Jamie is the brunette; Jessica is our little blonde."

Banks nodded. He always let Joetta have her way. Naming the twins was no exception.

"I'm going to spoil them rotten, sound good, Jessica and Jamie?"

Banks was so sweet. He was already a wonderful father.

Joetta felt hot tears roll down her cheeks. They were tears of joy. They would have to balance out the weight of her guilt and memory.

*The End*

The Kelly Sisters' Saga and the Story of the Gulfside Girls
Continues in *Gulfside Wish*.

**Summer Cottage Novels**

- Sandbar Sisters
- Sandbar Season
- Sandbar Summer
- Sandbar Storm
- Sandbar Sunrise

**Haven Beach Beachy Women's Fiction Series**

- Gulfside Girls
- Gulfside Inn
- Gulfside Secret
- Gulfside Wish
- Gulfside Sunset

## About the Author

Rebecca Regnier is an award-winning newspaper columnist, tv host, and former television news anchor. She lives in Michigan with her family and handsome dog. For all the latest from the beach and an exclusive bonus scene sign up for her newsletter or follow her on one of her socials. She loves to share laughs with her readers!

tiktok.com/@rebeccaregnier

facebook.com/rlregnier

instagram.com/rebeccaregnier

youtube.com/@RebeccaRegnierTV